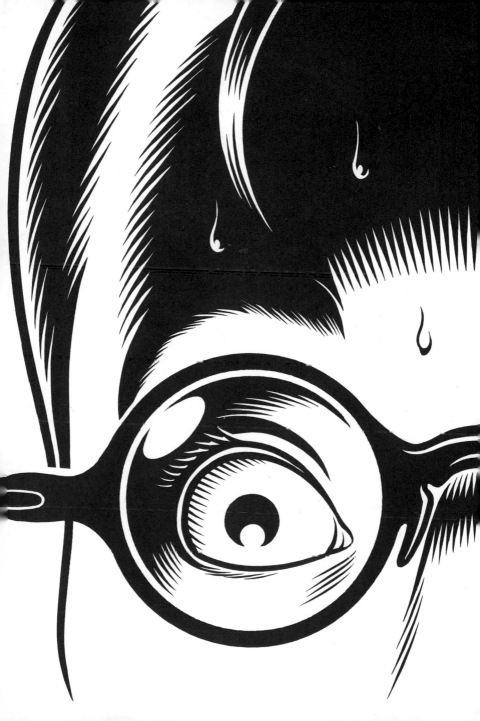

the

Lea

THE BOOK AFTER "T

CHI

pres

Sc

New York Lond

ners

: CHEESE MONKEYS"

 KIDD

ed by

n e r

oronto Sydney

CONTENTS

An idea ahead of its time, no matter what it is,
is *not* a good idea.

— No one you've ever heard of

———————————

Q: And babies?

A: And babies.

— The New York Times,
Nov. 25, 1969

1 9 6 1

WE'LL BE RIGHT BACK, AFTER THIS:

I was in the shower when I realized where I'd gone wrong. That's a cliché now, I know, but it wasn't then. Back then it was wildly new and *my* idea, and I would have copyrighted it had I foreseen it would become so popular, but well—as with *so* many things, who knew? Anyway, there I was, the water drilling away, its wet warmth my amniotic tide, the shower curtain a plastic, plaid uterine wall. Then it occurs to me, like a gift from God: Shoes are our friends.

Our *friends*.

Not just our acquaintances, the occasional giggly aunt and bald uncle over for dinner, the neighbors down the hall you have to say hello to—but the confidants we carefully screen and select over the course of a lifetime, our intimates. The ones who shield us from the slush, the sludge, the world's dirt underfoot.

But their love is not unconditional. We have a bargain to keep. If we are good to them, they'll give us everything they have, right down to their pocked, worn soles. Incredible.

Yes, this *was* news.

Clearly, I would have to change my strategy . . .

I.

BEFORE.

1 9 6 1

A U G U S T .

When Tip is standing in the doorway as he is right now, it can only mean one thing. I brace myself. He shouts, eyes pleading:

"Milk!"

After two and a half months, I'm starting to get used to it. Very jarring at first, but now I'm practically a pro. I counter, with excellent timing:

"Paint!"

Aha. Got him. He wasn't ready for *that.*

"Paint?"

I raise my head from the potato chip coupon I've been laying out with blue pencil for the past ten minutes and arch my right eyebrow, which is all he needs. Sketchy ignores us, as always.

"Faaassssssssinating." It's like a gas leak from Tip's mouth and he darts back down to his office.

And I am reminded, grateful: This *can* be a pretty fun place to work.

○ ○ ○

] 3 [

Who am I? I am Happy.

Not in any descriptive way, God knows—it's my name. A nickname, to be more precise, which I acquired relatively late in life, as those things go. From a teacher of mine in college, freshman year. And because of that it will always be who—not what—I am.

I wear it proudly, my sleeve's own Purple Heart.

Me: twenty-one years old, Caucasian male of mixed Anglo-Italian origin, olive-skinned, round tortoiseshell horn-rimmed glasses, hair sort of like Brandon De Wilde's in *Shane*, otherwise not interesting to look at. Or at least that's what the evidence would suggest.

Which is fine by me, because *I'm* the one doing the looking. I'm a graphic designer—I pretty much see the world as one great big problem to solve; one typeface, one drawing, one image at a time. Life is a lifelong assignment that must be constantly analyzed, clarified, figured out, and responded to appropriately.

I am inquisitive, though I hope not in any obnoxious way; and while I'm wary of any sort of unfamiliarity I am also quickly and easily bored by routine. I grew up in the eastern mid-Atlantic region of the United States, raised Protestant—the United Church of Christ—but have become very much of the "religion is the opiate of the people" school (the sole piece of common sense I gleaned from a course on Marxist theory, senior year), which of course I have elected to keep from my roundly nice, doting parents, lest they call the police. But I *am* close to my family, the way you are close to other people in a small crowded elevator that has temporarily stalled but will be moving any minute now. And as far as I was concerned, that minute was almost here.

Let's see, what else. I am convinced that ALL sports are a sanctioned form of mass-demonic worship, that cathedrals and museums have traded roles in the greater culture, and that Eve Arden is woefully underappreciated by society at large—as are comic books, malted milk, cracking your neck, secret decoder rings, glass tea kettles, whoopie pies, and television test patterns. And—ahem—graphic designers. That should do for now.

Wait, I'm forgetting something. Oh.

I do *not* write poetry.

But most of all: I am eager to start my career as a newly certified Bachelor of the Arts in Graphic Design, with a very specific goal—acquiring a job at the advertising agency of Spear, Rakoff & Ware; two states away, up in New Haven, Connecticut.

Why? Simple.

It's where Winter Sorbeck started. Long ago.

Now, yes—Winter, the teacher in question who christened me, my GD instructor during my first year at State—is a whole other story. And certainly one with no small amount of pain. But however bullying, severe, terror-inducing, and unnerving he was (and boy, was he), he was equal parts mesmerizing, eye-opening, inspiring, and brilliant. He was unlike any teacher I'd had, before or since. By the end of that spring semester he abruptly quit the faculty and vanished. I would have gladly dropped out to follow him anywhere, but no amount of amateur detective work revealed where that might be. So I bided my time, worked for the next three years to get my degree, and upon graduation decided: If I couldn't be where Winter was now, I'd go where he'd been. In the course of solving one of his earlier assignments I discovered that he started his career at Spear, Rakoff & Ware, and if that was good enough for him, it would be good enough for me.

Mandatory, actually.

And proving difficult. No surprise there—if Winter was anything, he was difficult, as would be anyplace associated with him. But no doubt worth the trouble. I approached the firm early, in March, three months before graduation. My initial inquiry went unanswered, as did my résumé (which could have won the *Collegian*'s annual First Fiction award), and the letter of recommendation I'd extorted from the dean's secretary. By May I was desperate, so I telephoned. The voice that greeted me hummed with the same welcome slow tone I knew from three years earlier, when I'd called for help on that gum wrapper label design problem for Winter. It was Milburne "Sketchy" Spear—the head of the art department. He didn't remember me and I didn't remind him—I wanted a clean start. The years had not changed his enthusiasm:

"Oh, you don't want to work here."

"Um, yes sir, I do."

"Really?"

"Yes sir."

Silence.

"Hello?"

"Sorry, I'm inking. Mind's a porch screen when I'm inking. I'm trying to do a crowd scene with a Number 5 Pedigree pen tip. Should be using a Radio 914. Doesn't really matter—can't draw anymore anyway, never could. God, I *stink*. Wouldn't you rather work someplace else? Where people didn't stink?"

What? "No sir, I'd like to work for your firm. You know, to sort of get my feet wet." Dreadful. Why did I say *that*?

"Heh." He sounded like a lawnmower trying to start. "Heh. That's what I thought. I mean, that's what *I* thought when I got here. You know when that was?"

"No. I—"

"You know dirt?"

"Dirt?"

"Dirt."

"Um, yes. Dirt."

"Well, I started here the year before they discovered it."

"I see."

"Heh."

"At least . . . it must have been spotless when you arrived."

"Heh-heh. Can you airbrush?"

"Yes, but—"

"Operate a photo-stat machine?"

"Did you receive my résu—"

"Do you know what I'm doing right now?"

"Uh, drawing a crowd scene with a . . . Number 5 Pedigree pen tip?"

"No, that's done. Now I'm trying to decide what kind of face the potato chip should have. That's always the question. Everything's a question."

"Pardon?"

"For this newspaper ad. A whole half-pager, due by five. Everyone signed off on it yesterday—the crowd, see, they've all filed out into the street to worship a giant potato chip."

"I see."

"Because it's a Krinkle Kutt. One of our biggest accounts."

"Right."

"Six stories tall." His tone was casual, as if he was telling me about his brother-in-law. "So, exactly what sort of expression should it have on its face? Because obviously, it's a very happy potato chip, to be a Krinkly Kollosus, and looked up to by all these tiny people, who adore it so."

"Well . . . it's obvious to me."

"That right?"

"It should look *chipper*."

"Heh."

"So to speak." Boy, was I making this up. Pure hokum. "You know, not so smug. He doesn't want to frighten everyone. I mean, *I'd* be wary of a protean jagged slab of tuber towering over my fellow citizens, our fate in his many, many eyes. Especially if he's been fried in lard. Which he has, I hope?"

"Heh. You *still* want to work here?"

"Definitely."

∘ ∘ ∘

But that was just the beginning. I managed to coax an appointment with Mr. Spear to show him my portfolio the first week of June; and while he did admit it wouldn't hurt to have some extra help, he also made it clear the decision on hires wasn't really his.

On the train to New Haven the day of our meeting, it dawned on me that this was hopeless.

Me, to me: *Do you realize what you are doing? This is what you are doing: You are going to a place you've never been, in a town that is totally unfamiliar, to meet with someone you don't know, in order to convince this person to pay you (regularly) to do something you've never done before.*

All that's missing is Sancho Panza at your side.

Agreed. But I had to try. Winter had, successfully.

Though now that I thought of it, he went to Yale. And I went to the opposite of Yale.

This bore more weight with each approaching stop.

"*. . . Fairfield, Bridgeport . . .*"

Of *course* they weren't going to take on anyone from a state university, much less one out of state.

"*. . . Stratford, Milford . . .*"

They obviously had some sort of direct-hire program from Yale, they'd be crazy not to.

"*. . . and New Haven. End of the line. All out.*"

What a waste of time, and sure to be humiliating. But I was used to that.

———

"This it?" asked the cabbie.

"I . . . guess so." Was it? The address matched, but still.

The drive from the beaux arts train station, so grand with its vaulted ceilings and terrazzo floors, took less than five minutes.

And now, as he drove off, I faced a study in contrasts: the probable office building of Spear, Rakoff & Ware. It wasn't at all what I'd pictured.

First, there were no columns in the lobby. Or trees, elevator attendants, cigar stands, shoe shine boys, or Gregory Peck. In fact, there was no lobby, at least none that I could make out from the sidewalk. There was a door. Period. It was black, cast iron, and apparently bolted shut. The only other advertising agency I'd ever seen was the one from *The Man in the Gray Flannel Suit,* and though I realized that was in New York (and fake New York at that), I also thought it might have represented some kind of national standard. Nope.

Before me stood a weathered four-story Victorian brick cottage on Trumbull Street. A plaque welded to the right of the entrance announced itself as the town's first firehouse "in the years when Dickens declared Hillhouse Avenue (a five-minute walk away) the most beautiful street in America."

Probably because he'd just come from this one.

Parked in the garage off to the left, where one pictured a once trusty horse-drawn water wagon waiting to race to its next bucket brigade, was an Olympic-size '59 Cadillac convertible the color of raw veal. And it had about as much room to move as a fatted calf—the back end of it jutted out of the garage, blocking half the sidewalk. The top was down and the eggshell blue upholstery, immaculate on the driver's side, was, on the passenger seat, mauled to a relish of leather and foam.

I rang the bell—not really a bell at all, but a chrome box with rounded edges and vertical slits, hovering over a red Bakelite button. I pressed it again.

Static. "Yes?" A woman's voice, swarming with electrons. Sounded like she was counties away.

"Is this Spear, Rakoff and Ware?"

"Yes?"

Could she hear me? I pushed the button a third—

"Please stop that."

Yipes. "Sorry. I'm here to see Mr. Spear, please."

"Do you have an appointment?"

"Oh, yes ma'am. He's expecting me." I gave her my name. Waited.

And waited. Then

"*ZZZZZZZZZZZAAAATTT!!!*"

It was the door—apparently several thousand volts

of electricity were coursing through the handle. I couldn't bring myself to touch it.

Finally, it popped open and a lady with ice-white hair the shape and texture of spun sugar stuck her head out and looked at me—the way a duchess would notice a stain on her bedsheets.

"Isn't this working?" she snapped, glaring at the buzzer with her pretty knife of a face, ready to have the knob drawn and quartered. Her eyes glowed with the fact that her perfect hands and their attending scarlet talons were made for better things than this, than for opening doors for *me*.

"I, I don't know."

She sighed mightily and withdrew and let it begin to close. I caught it just before it latched, and followed her in.

The reception area had one small couch—a rounded Machine Age number made of worn gray suede and aluminum tubing. I gingerly sat on it; me—a terrible intruder, a twig in the spokes of this agency's mighty wheel. The ceiling was double-height, with three windows on the second-floor level (apparently inaccessible to cleaners) facing a balcony with offices behind it. The center of the room was pierced by a polished stainless-steel cylindrical beam that ran from floor to ceiling.

This firehouse smelled . . . of smoke.

A bowl of potato chips on the coffee table in front of me rested atop five back issues of *Advertising Production Techniques Weekly*. A handwritten and folded piece of paper, like a place card at a dinner party, had been positioned in front of it and said DO NOT TOUCH. The secretary promptly forgot I existed, having clamped an operator's headset onto her comely skull and set to typing with the fury of an aerial machine gunner laying waste to a squadron of Sopwith Camels. Another bowl of potato chips sat next to her typewriter, with its own warning to stay clear of it.

I waited helplessly for something to happen, sorrier by the second. What could I have been thinking? How could I have thought I'd ever be of any use to anyone here? Those chips sure looked good. Minutes crawled by like desert-marooned cartoon characters. Thirsty. And now I wanted to eat a potato chip more than I wanted to keep breathing. My tie was tightening around my throat, the armpits in my good Arrow shirt grew wet and hot under my confirmation blazer, and my new cordovan Bass Weejuns were strangling my feet. The next train back left in forty minutes. I was going to be on it.

"What's the matter, sitting on a tack?"

A voice with the timbre of a bell—bright, piercing, capable of alarm. He'd appeared magically to my left—a tall boy-man in white shirtsleeves and a thin crimson tie, dark gray trousers—he was lithe and angular and trying to keep still. His wire-rim glasses were lit by eyes that looked at you and somewhere behind you and someplace beyond that, to be sure. They flanked a beaky nose that didn't fit in with the rest of his face at all—an uninvited guest to the party of his features.

The yellow legal pad clutched tight in his right hand bore what looked like obsessively scrawled notes for the Encyclopedia Britannica. Or an A-bomb.

I started to explain myself. "I—"

Sotto voce, to me: "Don't tell me Preechy left you here to fend for your*self.*" He glanced back to the secretary's desk, which was mounted on a platform perched a good two feet above the floor, accessible by steps. He must have thought I was someone else, talking to me like this.

"Well, I'm here to see Mr. Spear. I—"

"Oh, that pasty, slacked-titted harpy." Louder, to her, "Miss Preech? Woo-hoo! Darling." Tilting his head to me. "Has he been seen to?"

The woman glowered at him poisonously and shouted, her hands never stopping their mad staccato dance, "Mr. Spear was called AWAY. He will be back SHORTLY."

Under his breath, eyes sideways: "*Such* a gorgon. Silver bullets would be useless."

I caught myself in a small guffaw—just what he wanted. He was performing. He switched the pad to his left hand, extended the other.

"I'm Tip. Tip Skikne."

"Tip?"

"As in 'of the iceberg'. "

"Oh. I'm . . . Happy."

"Well, good for you. I'm morose. But I mask it *beautifully.* "

I explained my nickname.

"Oh, how sad. Mine's a nickname too—'Thomas' sounds too much like an English muffin. Cup of coffee? Our Mr. Spear is probably taking one of his copyrighted 'inspirational walks.' He seemed eager for diversion. Could be a while."

"Oh, thanks. Yes, please. And . . ." I didn't know how to ask it.

He looked differently at me all of a sudden. Seriously. Professionally. "You want a potato chip," he said slyly, "don't you? Tell the truth."

"Actually, yes. How did you—"

"And before you came in here it was the furthest thing from your mind, especially at this hour, wasn't it."

"Well, yes."

"Thank GOD. That was the whole idea. You *see?* I'm really onto something." His face lit up. "CRISPY!"

"What?"

"Don't be frightened. Just say the first word that pops into your head when I say CRISPY!"

Whoa.

"CRISPY!"

"Uh, 'Cornies,' I guess."

"Cornies? What the hell is that?" A puzzled look, bringing up the pad with a jolt. He urgently started writing.

My eyes went to Miss Preech, grateful to see her oblivious—I was about to bare something personal. For some reason, I knew I could open up to this guy: "Crispy Cornies was my favorite cereal in . . . the fifth grade. You know, Kenny Kernel sang the theme song.

'*Crispy Cornies crunch like COOKies! Crunch-crunch-crunch, a whole BIG bunch!*'" I was actually singing—it had come to that. I caught myself, mortified: "It was Flash Gordon's favorite."

Scribbling, scribbling. "Mmhmm, the cereal—was it good? Tasting, I mean."

"No, not really. Too mealy, too mapley. Turned the milk into a muddy sop. But it had the best toys, so there was no question."

"Go on."

"Well, they made a Ming the Merciless death ray you could cut from the box and construct entirely out of cardboard, mucilage, three rubber bands, and ten, ten? hairpins." It actually worked—on tiny, doomed baby field mice plucked from the woods behind our house. "Didn't you ever try them?"

"I'm Canadian," he said.

Oh. Maybe that explained it, this immediate familiarity. They just don't tell you these things in school. "Wow."

"I know. I pass for an actual human being. But I rarely try." Whether he tried or not, the effect was convincing. He radiated a strategic urgency, as if he was working on ten things at once in his mind. He belonged here, no doubt about that. I studied him as he flipped through several leaves of the legal pad and made more notations. Then he put it down, picked up the bowl of potato chips from the coffee table with both hands, and raised it to me, like a grail full of Incan blood.

"Help yourself."

Maybe it was just me, but the way he said it . . . it meant more than it usually does.

○ ○ ○

"You see, *that's* what interests me." Tip Skikne's office, on the first floor, had a real, tennis-playing squirrel in it. "It's fascinating." A stuffed one, mounted on an ashtray, on the right corner of his desk. But reclining in his chair, hands behind his head, that wasn't what he was referring to. "You associate 'crispy' not with a natural entity— 'corn,' say," eyes glued to something on the ceiling, "but with a completely artificial construct that's been placed into your mind, your memory, by other *people* . . ." The squirrel sported Lacoste whites and clutched a tiny racket, suspended forever in mid-serve. "By adding three letters to the word 'corn,' it's no longer made by God, it's made by man. Amazing." Mounted on its left leg, the right leg was bent and raised behind him. Perfectly balanced— flawless form. "And that's not even why I asked you to free-associate in the first place." I wondered where the ball was. Probably buried under the mound of cigarette butts. "But such is serendipity. I doubt it will help me with my current adversitorial dilemma, but there it is. Am I boring you?" Now he leaned forward, staring.

"Huh? Oh no, not at all. I was just admiring your squirrel."

He folded his hands and calmly placed them on the desk. "Yes, that's Victor. Get it? So now, what can I do for you?"As if the last ten minutes hadn't happened.

What? I finished chewing a potato chip, swallowed. Those were good. "I'm waiting to see Mr. Spear, actually, remember?" I set down my coffee mug. "Maybe I should go back to—"

"Right, yes, yes." Glasses in one hand, rubbing his eyes with the other. "No. I can't leave you in the clutches of . . ." He thought better of what he was going to say and looked over at my portfolio case. "And you're here to see Sketchy about . . ."

Sketchy. "A job. I just graduated. I—"

"That sneak. He didn't tell me they were looking for—"

"Well, that's because they—you're . . . probably not. See, I just sort of called him."

"Right. Could I have a look?" He gestured to my case.

Here we go, I'd better start getting used to it. "Sure."

He untied it and looked at the first page. "How interesting. What . . . is that?"

"It's a pencil drawing."

"That I can see. Of what? It looks like—"

"It's a kiwi," I deadpanned. "A decapitated kiwi. And a wing-tip shoe."

He was frozen, in either awe or pity.

"I did it in freshman Still Life. I always thought it looked like they were having a conversation, so later, for my portfolio, I turned it into a cartoon." I reached down and opened a flap beneath it to reveal the caption:

Help me get a head, and I'll help you get a foot in the door.

He smirked. "You didn't go to school around here, did you?"

"You could say that." I was starting to produce flop sweat. I changed the subject. "So, may I ask, what *is* your current adver, advers . . ."

"Adversitorial dilemma—my own term." Proud as punch. "Well," he said, resting his folded forearms on the drawing as if it were a diner placemat, "it's no big deal. Or maybe it is. It's just an *idea* I had." He said the word "idea" the way most other people would say "dead child." "See, I keep trying to tell them—it's really very simple: Ads don't sell products."

I didn't quite know what to say to that. We *were* sitting in an ad agency. Where he worked.

"*Stores* sell products. Right?" One of those T H I N K signs hung on the wall to the left, onto which he'd taped a piece of notebook paper, scrawled in red crayon with the word *"Again!"* "At least nod your head up and down. Even if you don't mean it."

I did so.

"Bless you. So, an ad for potato chips shouldn't be actually trying to sell you potato chips, should it? Because the ad itself can't give you the potato chips."

Silence.

"It should be selling you a *need* for potato chips.

That it can give you. Right?"

Hmmm. "Rrrright."

"Of course. So I said . . ." He spread his hands, conducting a secret symphony, "let's do ads that say no one is allowed to *have* potato chips—you know, show big, glorious pictures of salty, crispy, golden goodness—and say . . ." He paused, then, loudly, "YOU CAN'T HAVE THEM. Genius? Genius." He sighed and let the music die in his head. "And they look at me like I've just asked them to ball my mother."

A vision of Winter applauding in the classroom, with his all-too-rare grin of fiendish approval, flashed in my head. "I had a teacher once who would have loved that idea. Who's the them?"

"The Krinkle people. The Krinklies. One of our biggest accounts, for decades."

"Oh."

"Actually, it's not them. I hardly ever get to talk to them, it's Pr—" We could hear the front door down the hall open and close. A man's gentle, mumbled voice. "But I'm pummeling you with this, a total stranger. My apologies."

"Not at all, it's—"

"Sketchy's here. C'mon." He folded up the portfolio flaps, got up, and motioned me out of the room.

"Maybe you can get ahead."

By the time we reached Mr. Spear's office two flights up, he was hunched over his drawing board, deep in his chores. Through the open doorway: it was a tableaux from the cover of *The Saturday Evening Post.* The ceiling was arched and highest in the middle—we were in the attic, which likely served as the firemen's dorms. A window in the shape of a half-moon, flat side down and divided like the sections of an orange, rose from the floor to chest height and spanned about six feet in the center of the facing wall. The very air seemed a good forty years old—not because it was musty (okay, it was, a little), but because it appeared that nothing in it had been disturbed since Prohibition, or before. A glass shelf of old Felix the Cat dolls of all shapes, sizes, and materials jutted out from the wall behind him, each one looking over his shoulder to see what he was doing. I wanted to join them—to be one of them. Two green-globed Victorian brass architectural lamps flanked the blond oak drafting table, vice-clamped at the top and bent over and scanning the surface like extras from *The War of the Worlds.* Spear was in profile to us, the Sherlock Holmes pipe in his teeth leaking a cherry musk that put me back at my grandpa's. Arden and Ohman's recording of "Maple Leaf Rag" tumbled out of the hand-crank phonograph in the corner and colored everything sepia. The steel beam that I'd seen in the reception room continued up here through the middle of the floor and on up to the roof. There was a circular patch of concrete around the base like a plug in the middle of the wooden boards.

Milburne Spear himself was both what I'd pictured and yet a surprise because of it. He didn't seem so much like a draughtsman as he did a watchmaker, carefully constructing, adjusting. In fact, he could have been the son of Santa Claus, a good twenty years from taking over the family business, just as soon as he grew a beard and put on a gut. Round face and head, with graying hair thinned at the top and crew-cut army style. A strong, hearty man. But he was delicate and sturdy at the same time. The sturdy part was physical—barrel-chested, bushy-browed, his shirt-sleeves rolled up past his elbows. His left forearm, easily the width of a ham hock, lay across the board in front of him, a furry blockade to anyone trying to see what he was doing. But the delicate part emerged from his work. Whatever he was rendering, it had his undivided attention, and I soon realized we could have stood inside the doorway for hours and he never would have seen us. Tip finally broke the ice.

"Ahem. Sketch?"

"Hmm?" He pushed up his spectacles, tiny ovals of glass connected by a thin gold strip across the bridge of his nose.

"Sketcher, your appointment is here. Mr. Happy."

Head up, confused, then, "Oh!" Terror, as if remembering he left the gas burner on at home. Or just stepped on a kitten. "Wasn't that tomorrow?"

He was gracious and very attentive and obviously couldn't have cared less about my portfolio at all.

Until he saw Baby Laveen.

"Golly, he's a corker. You do *that*?"

"Yessir." My own comic strip character. I wasn't even going to include him, and now thanked God strenuously that I had. Baby Laveen was an infant dressed as a grown man—in fact even though he looked like he was literally born yesterday, in all other respects he lived and functioned among adults, who didn't seem any the wiser and respected him in his job as assistant district attorney in the mid-Atlantic city called Doddsville. Spear was transfixed. Tickled.

"Heh-HEH. You did this in school?"

"Yes." Officially, no. There was no cartooning class at State, surprise surprise. It wasn't something I seriously thought about pursuing full-time, but as a hobby it was a hoot. "I mean, I was in school when I did that, yes, but it wasn't part of the curriculum. It was just for fun It's based on . . . someone I used to know."

"*This* is someone you used to know? A baby in a business suit?"

"It's hard to explain. But yes. I knew his . . . mother. Just something I wanted to do. S'pretty dumb, I know."

"No, not dumb. He's *pesky.*" His face could have been mine when I was five, lying on my belly on the living room carpet on Sunday afternoon with the funnies spread out everywhere. "You've figured out his eyes. That's the hardest part."

Wow. "You think? Oh, thanks. It's really all about proportion. And whether or not the eyes should be open circles, or filled in. Or just slits. And how close they are to the nose. But you know all that. Don't you think Harold Gray changed everything, with Orphan Annie?"

A grunt. "He got a lot of it from McCay. Most everyone has."

"Who?"

"You don't know Winsor McCay? Little Nemo?" Scandalized. Stern with me: "*In Slumberland.*"

"Oh, our paper at home doesn't carry him."

He very politely and ineffectively tried to look like I hadn't just said something really, really stupid. Then he pretended I hadn't said anything at all, and turned the page . . .

. . . to my sketches for ketchup and mustard dispensers. Shaped like torsos.

"Those would be molded out of soft plastic," I said. "Like what they use for Frisbees, only more flexible? People should be able to squeeze them—I think that's the future. We shake things—bottles, now, because they're glass. But at some point I think they won't be, because glass breaks and doesn't give. Plastic's the opposite. I think things should be squeezed. *I'd* rather be squeezed than shaken. Wouldn't you?" Good Lord, what was wrong with me?

Our eyes locked in an ersatz standoff, and his crippled smile and his eyebrows reaching for his scalp betrayed the thought that one half of me was starkers and the other was the sanest person in the world.

"Heh, yep." He closed the leather flaps.

"I-" I stammered, desperate, desperate, "Mr. Spear,

] 2 4 [

is there any chance that, you could—"

"Well, like I said," gazing at his shoes, "I could use the help, and we've got a desk." He looked over at a small drawing table in the corner I hadn't noticed before. It was smudged with ink and dotted with mummified bits of masking tape and it was all I ever wanted and its beauty mocked me. My pulse went from 45 to 78 rpm. "But I'll have to teach you how to use a ruling pen. You're holding it wrong. You a lefty?" I nodded. "Thought so—you're overcompensating, and the uniformity of the line thickness is suffering. Need to keep your elbow down, close to your side." He gestured and dropped his head again. "But Mrs. Rakoff'll have to approve a new hire. She's the boss lady. Can you," hesitant, slightly tensing, "can you come back tomorrow morning?"

Rats. Another four hours up and back in the train? Come on, I'm so *close*. "Actually, is there any way I could see her today? I'll wait however long. It's just that tomorrow . . , I have another interview." At my dentist's, where he would inevitably ask me why I haven't been getting at the backs of my rear molars, so it wasn't a lie.

"Hmm." Even tenser. "Wait here a sec." He took my portfolio. After five minutes, he still hadn't returned, so I screwed up the nerve to stand and look at what was on his drawing table.

Holy smoke. The work surface itself was filthy, but taped to it was a pristine piece of illustration board, emblazend with a new pen-and-ink full-page Krinkle

Kutt layout. Near completion. To say it was only a newspaper ad was to say that the Bayeux Tapestry was simple reportage. Under a script banner that read KRINKLE IS KING!, this time His Highness Potato Chip loomed over an enslaved realm of hundreds of mini-pretzels, a networked multitude, each in a tiny harness connected to a massive chariot bearing their enormous conqueror, beaming in tater triumph. It was the snack version of Exodus, a panorama of—

"Don't look at that." In the doorway. Not angry—no . . . embarrassed. Embarrassed to be alive. "I can't draw."

Right. And Sinatra can't sing. Was he serious?

"Please."

Oh. That face: a rictus of apology, shame. Yes, he was. It made me want to fix the world. For him.

"Uh, sorry. I was just sneaking a look. This is . . . incredible. Just breathtaking. I mean . . . "

It was like I'd slapped him.

"She can see us. I think," he said, not at all convincingly, and motioned for me to follow. We went downstairs, to the second floor.

I'd never seen an office door quite like it, not in the art department at State or anywhere else. It was pink. Even the lettering on the rippled glass.

MILDRED MITCHELL RAKOFF

PRESIDENT

And I mean PINK. A pink like we could get irradiated from standing here for more than five minutes. Sketch knocked gingerly, as if he was reading my mind.

"Yes?" From inside. Muffled yet piercing.

"It's me." He shyly turned the knob, cracked the door, eased in, closed it. In the hallway, I strained to hear, but could only make out parts of her end of the discussion. Which were not encouraging. The phrases "second thoughts," "I know what I said but," "we don't need to," and most oddly, "talk to the shoe!" told me I'd be on the 2:58, one-way after all. Crap. I was almost there.

Dammit.

Then the door opened and a beet-faced Sketch came out and was about to say something when another face—a furious roil of matriarchic agitation and withered glamour—appeared behind him, shrieking, "Oh, and Milby, Dicky says someone named Lenny from Krinkle said that—"

I almost gasped. Almost. But Mom raised me better than that. I just gaped.

"—in that last thing you did, the thing from Tuesday? In the *Register*? He said—"

And stared. And you would have, too, because:

"—could we make the pretzels look less salty this time? He says they look saltier than the chips, and—"

1) An adult, especially of what appeared to be her advanced age and breeding, just should NOT venture out in public with that many Band-Aids on her head.

"—that sends the wrong message. It doesn't say—"

2) Once it's become clear that the sun is destroying your skin, it would probably be a better idea to wear a turtleneck. Not a sleeveless V-neck Dior paired with pink and green flower-print pants.

"—'eat me'. It's just going to make people thirsty and they'll—"

3) Expensive, flawlessly tailored clothing will only throw your . . . appearance into sharper relief, especially when you're starting from somewhere between Barbara Stanwyck and The Thing.

"—turn the page and buy a Coke. Okay?"

and 4) Logic dictates that presidents of advertising agencies *must* make enough money to buy extravagant luxuries, like food. Right? She was going to have to try some. Soon, before collapsing into a bone pile.

"Oh. Oh my."

Oops. This, this Lily Pulitzer wraith, had me in her sights. I had to get out of there.

"Is this, is . . . ? " And she, *whup*, clutched my chin and turned my head from side to side, like it was a crenshaw melon she was inspecting at the IGA. "Is this the *boy?*"

Bloodless claws. I wasn't sure. Was I? Sketch must have nodded.

"Oh, that's . . . marvelous," she hissed, and unhanded me and turned her laser eyes on Spear and yanked him back into her office. The door snapped shut to furious murmurs.

And then, like a jack-in-the-box he popped out—years obviously gone from his life, and he said, like magic:

"C-can you start Tuesday? Seventy-five a week?"

Oh, could I. He led us down the hallway.

"Mr. Spear," I started, as we plodded down the staircase, "can you tell me why—"

No words left in him, he stopped on the landing and took a moment to write something down on an index card from his front shirt pocket, folded and handed it to me—in a scrupulous grab, behind his back, out of view of the secretary. Who wasn't looking anyway.

"Read it on the train. We'll talk."

I palmed it. "Right. I can't thank you enough. I—"

"Miss Preech will get you a cab."

She was typing again. Now, obviously she was a stranger to me, but I already suspected that even if I were to lie on the floor in front of her with a meat axe growing out of my head, in a pool of my own hot hemoglobin, the probability of Miss Preech calling me an ambulance would be remote in the extreme—much less a cab, right now. "Thanks, thanks, Mr. Spear," I said groggily. I rang one for myself from the corner payphone.

On the train, safely speeding home, I pulled out Sketchy's message: a fortune cookie slip that would determine my future for *real.* Did I really want to know? I kept it closed all the way to Stamford. Then I just couldn't stand it anymore and shut my eyes, opened it, ready for the oracle's wisdom:

**CAN'T EXPLAIN RIGHT NOW.
HAVE YOU EVER USED AN ERASER GUARD?
JUST ASKING. SORRY.
SEE YOU SOON.**

It was all in a cartoon speech balloon, coming out of the mouth of . . . Baby Laveen, pleading to the judge. Perfect to the detail.

Perfect like I could never, ever draw him.

o o o

"And here's where—*nuts*. We're out of atomic teat." Tip, in a short-sleeved ash gray madras dress shirt that revealed skinny arms as pale and hairless as zucchini squash, waved the empty powdered milk box, lamenting. "Rats. I love this stuff. It makes my coffee *experimental.* It gives me hope. Miss Preech!" My first day, in the middle of the unofficial office tour. Mr. Spear wasn't in yet. In fact, it was ten to nine and aside from Tip, Miss Preech, and me, neither was anyone else. Tip and I were in the little galley kitchen off the pantry, where they made their coffee. I mean, where *we* made it. God, it was just too amazing.

"Miss Preech!" he shouted at the ceiling.

"What?!" she crowed from her desk.

"Darling, we're out of powdered milk." His voice was all knives.

"No. We are not." Hers were sharper.

"Sweetness, we ARE." Eyes clenched. This guy was a card, a real Franklin Pangborn Jr., but not someone I'd want to be on the wrong side of, I could tell already.

And then, the rapid-fire click of high heels, angry on the linoleum floor. She rounded the corner, thrust out a new box, and slammed it down on the counter. *Wham!*

And back to her desk.

I offered, weakly, "You, you two don't seem to, like each other."

His eyes bloomed in protest. "Nonsense. Why, there's nothing in the world I wouldn't do for her, and there's nothing she wouldn't do for me." He hurled the old box into the corner trash can with considerable force. "In fact, we spend our whole *lives* doing nothing for each other."

"Oh."

He jimmied open the metal pouring spout and shook a small blizzard of Bessie's Evaporated Moo Juice into his cup. "She's the princess *and* the pea." He sighed. "I've spent some time behind that desk myself, so I know why she's so dreadful. But it doesn't make it any easier. She hates that I got a rung up."

"Why?"

"Oh, what does it matter? Sugar?" Pouring my java. "What she needs is a man."

"Really? She's so pretty."

"So's a poinsettia. Ever taste one?"

The front door buzzed. In walked Sketchy.

"Morning."

Tip handed me my coffee, lit up his Marlboro. "Well, I'll leave you to your labors." Nodding his head to Spear, "Sketch, sir? Krinkle meeting at eleven, yes? In the conference room?"

"What? Sure." Then, to me, "Well, hello. You made it? Heh."

"Yes." God, I'd hoped so. "Yes, I did."

"Good deal. See ya upstairs."

"Yes sir." And I bolted to the steps, took them two at a time, careful not to slosh the coffee.

The art department. It all looked so different now—the two drawing tables scarred with countless X-Acto marks, the piles of scattered scrap artboard, wads of tape that were overshot to the trash can and dotted the wall behind it like measles. The magic of seeing it for the first time was gone, but replaced by something even more alluring—the promise of inclusion among its details. I saw a stage set that I was now invited to climb up onto. I wasn't in the audience anymore, I was a player. Maybe just a member of the chorus, but still.

And yet it was clear from the start that Sketch was uncomfortable having assistants or delegating tasks, no matter how much he claimed to need an "extra pair of hands." What he meant was an extra pair of his own, not someone else's.

Nonetheless, "Let's have you rule out some mechanical boards. The *Register* has their own done up, but they're not worth the, well, the you-know-what they print 'em on, sorry. You good at key lines?"

Gulp. "That depends. What are they?"

He chuckled, then winked. "Oh, you'll see."

Sketch. He was the most astonishing contradiction of components I'd ever encountered. Shy yet fiercely communicative when putting an idea into your head. Vocally astringent regarding his own abilities but not to the point that he couldn't produce—he was as prolific an artist (yes, an artist, and I never use the term, especially regarding people I like) I've ever seen. But I could feel it: everything he sketched, penciled, inked, made—was a payment, one he could scarcely afford; as if it physically hurt him to put pencil to paper. Yet that only seemed to spur him on, to live far beyond his means. He was unable not to. For Sketch, to draw was to breathe, and so the air became lead—silvery in the right light, dark soot in the wrong; heavy, slick, and malleable—into shapes he brought together in glorious orchestration, with a child's eye and a rocket scientist's precision, all fortified by a furious melancholy, a quiet engine of sourceless shame and humility.

When it came to another's work, he longed to praise it but then couldn't resist critiquing it all within an inch of its life, analyzing deficiencies with uncontrollable abandon and laser accuracy. He was as sharp as his Radio 914 pen nibs, and as pointed.

And then he'd apologize. Oh, he would *apologize:* Oh my GOD, forgive me, please don't hate me, I'm SORRY, don't listen to me, why am I saying things, what do I know, I don't know *anything,* why do you listen to me you should just tell me to shut UP, I'm awful, *forgive* me, you hate me, don't you? Tell the truth. Please don't hate me. Please don't. Please?

That first day, we started off with the concept of the blue pencil.

"You ever use one of these?"

It looked like a normal one, except the lead was the color of a robin's egg. "Yes." No—don't. "No."

"Heh. Well, this is a lot to take in, but here goes: everything we do gets shot by a high-contrast camera in the basement here called a stat machine. I'll show you that, later. But basically, this camera sees only black and white—no shades of gray unless we use a Zipatone pattern. I'll show you that later, too. The main thing is that red registers as black, and blue as white. For all cameras. That's why you have a red light in a darkroom when you make photo prints. But with blue whatever you draw is invisible. So we use that to do the basic layout and then ink over it. The camera only sees the ink on the board and shoots it as line art. You see?"

"Wow."

"What."

"I sure could have used one of those in school. I used to draw everything in regular pencil first and then went back and erased it all after the ink was dry."

"We all did. Actually," he lowered his voice, even though no one could have possibly heard us, or cared, "you're not really supposed to render with blue pencil—it's just meant for key lines and such. But one day a couple of years ago I was really pressed for time on a Krinkle full-pager and thought, Hell, why not, and drew the whole damn thing in non-photo blue. No erasing! Saved me a good half hour. Never looked back." He pulled a sheaf of paper from the side table next to his board.

"These are sizes for the next month. If you could set these up, that'd be great." And then he added, with a sincerity that told me who he was—I'll never forget it: "Do ya mind?"

Mind? "No sir, not at all."

"Thanks, kid."

And so I started ruling out mechanical boards, readying them for Sketch to fill. For anyone else this might have have been tedious grunt work. But not for me. Not then. I was finally putting pencil to paper for a real reason. A purpose. For me it was heaven. Blue heaven.

At around half-past noon, Tip's head popped in the doorway.

"Do you have lunch plans?"

Was he joking? Hard to tell. "No. You?"

"Mory's. I'm a member. One thirty? Sketch, is that all right? Wanna come?"

"Heh. Huh?" Lost in Krinkle-land. "No, you go ahead."

It was an "eating club" on the edge of the Yale campus. Dickens would have loved it and probably did. White clapboard, black shutters. Discreet brass plaque on the door with the "Mory's" name. Inside: photos on the walls of sports teams and captains, crew or baseball or tennis—grimly bright-eyed in yesteryear's outfits that looked now like an odd pajama party. Ranks of the hopeful young—class of '15, some of whom probably jumped off windowsills on Wall Street after the Crash; or class of '40, more than one of them washed up on Omaha Beach. The team captain posed against a mock rail fence, already the master of a jaunty look he'd wear years later in boardroom or bank vault.

From the ceiling oars hanging in rows, painted with the legend of that year's victory over Harvard in the Thames regatta: 1952, Yale 21:04, Harvard 22:34, etc. Trophies left behind by the young, who, fresh from the first flush of victory, had no idea where they were finally headed.

So this was planet Yale. Where I was an alien.

Our table, as were all the others, was gouged with initials and dates and Latin boasts, the "Kilroy Was Here" of those who weren't anymore. Our fossilized penguin of a waiter handed us dog-eared menus engraved with a script type that did its elegant best to hold off against years of grease and gravy stains. Tip ordered clam chowder, steak Diane, and a Dewar's.

I asked for a club sandwich. And a lemon Coke.

He laughed. When the drinks arrived Tip raised his glass to me. I met him with a clink.

"To your first day," he said, "in this dreadful business."

Hmm. "Oh, don't say that. Don't you like advertising?"

He grinned. "Well, I've always loved interrupting. I'm made for it. Ask anyone. And that *is* what we do."

"It is?"

"Of course, it's the whole nature of the biz. Ads are interruptions—but interruption as main topic. Look at magazines. Look at television. On television, in fact, it goes even further—the ads are far more important than the TV shows."

"That's ridiculous."

"Is it? The shows are interrupted by the commercials. But," he hiked his eyebrow in an *arc de triomphe,* "the commercials are *never* interrupted."

Yes, I thought, because they're so short. I didn't say it. Instead, "How many have you worked on?"

"How many what?"

"TV commercials. I'll bet they're fun."

"Oh, how sweet. Yes, I'll bet they are. Will let you know if I ever find out."

"But don't you—"

"Buddy boy, we're not in that league." He drained his scotch on the rocks. "We're mom-and-pop. Just Mom actually, for some time now."

"Mrs. Rakoff."

"Mmmm. Mimi."

"Mimi?"

"Yes, as in," he sucked in his cheeks and made a vulture voice and poked himself in the chest, "Me! Me!"

I recounted our rather odd meeting.

"Pretty typical, I'm afraid." He tried to coax more

liquid from his glass, got ice instead. "She doesn't *go* to extremes; she *lives* there."

"Is she . . . good at what she does?"

He cracked a cube between his teeth and looked out the window, seeking something in the sky. A star to wish on? A gargoyle on the Sterling Library across the street? "Actually," he sighed, his eyes back to me, betraying a search in vain, "she would be enormously *improved* by death."

• • •

It only took five days to find an apartment, what with most of the students gone for the summer. Tip was all too happy to help look during lunch breaks. He'd had his run-ins with real-estate agents and wanted to spare me the trouble.

"You'll be raped otherwise, trust me. Those people will poke out your eyes and make love to your skull. And send you a bill. Oh, no. You're a *child.*"

I settled on a furnished third-floor walk-up on Cottage Street off Orange, just a ten-minute bike ride from the office. It was half of the top floor of a large Victorian house that had been divided into flats. Mine was four small rooms accessed by an outdoor staircase added on to the side—sort of a reverse fire escape. I'm a nester by nature, but here I wanted to start anew, with few possessions and almost no furniture. The rooms—with their threadbare faux Oriental throw rugs and shopworn velveteen armchairs—due to the previous grad-school tenants, smelled like an old wet pizza box. Which I found to be not altogether unpleasant.

I amazed myself at how quickly I wanted to take to New Haven. I'm usually not good with change, but it was a college town after all, and that dynamic was welcome and familiar. The difference, of course, was that this college was one I hadn't dared dream of becoming part of. And yet here I was, a foundling on the doorstep of Mother Yale. Was I trespassing? Maybe. But I wasn't alone. The rift between Town and Gown was a chasm you couldn't jump, like nothing I'd ever, ever seen before. Back at State, we shared a sense that even the most grimy, bloated old sot asleep at his hooch down at the Skeller could be roused with a poke to sing the school fight song, if that's what it took to win the big game. We fed on the underlying "we're all in this together." In New Haven it was more like occupied France, but no Allies to the rescue this time. Yale itself was outwardly charming and stately—neo-Gothic colleges that looked as if Hansel and Gretel were on the planning committee, all presided over by the magnificent Harkness Tower. But take one step over the campus line and you were outside the fortress with the enemy advancing. And therein lay my predicament: I certainly didn't belong inside the walls, and on the other side of them I wasn't really one of the locals, either. Was I?

But harder still to get used to was the giddy reality of actually having a *job*. I was paid to make *things*. Each morning around nine I'd buzz myself in with a key and slink past the wilting eyes of Miss Preech and wonder why she didn't drop what she was doing and call the police. And then I'd pop up the stairs, and more often than not Sketchy would already be there, with the phonograph leaking its tired, wonderful ragtime into the warmth of the slatted morning light. And he'd look up (either from his work or the early edition of the paper, depending on deadlines) and throw me half a smile and a wink.

And I'd be home.

I learned more that first week than I did in four years of college. To wit:

1) How to hold a pencil. "Not so tight. You're strangling it. Let it do what it wants, stray a little. Give it permission."

2) How to hold a pen. "Ink, on the other hand, is sneaky—needs discipline. LOTS of it. Let it know you're the boss. You want it to do what it doesn't want to. Tough. When you're in control, it will do it."

3) How to sit. "Go ahead and slouch. Life is short, now you are, too. Heh."

4) How to use a brush. Truth to tell, I never really did come close to mastering this one, but I did start to get the idea of it. "It's a pen, really. Just a fluid one." Sketch could make lines and shapes with a brush that you'd swear were stamped by a machine. Remarkable.

And the biggie:

5) How to draw a straight line. "Pretend it exists already and just trace it. Keep your wrist stiff but let your arm glide. Try to forget that straight lines are

truly unnatural—created by humans to convey a sense of the mechanical, which isn't human at all. Think of food."

"Food?"

"Something yummy. Spicy."

"Why?"

"Because you have to think of *some*thing. Don't you like food? Cats then. Fluffy cats. Something."

"Why don't I think about drawing the line correctly?"

"Try it."

He was right, of course—now I was thinking about it to the point of stage fright and the result was not uniform in width, slightly slanting downward to the left, and dotted with blobs. All of which I would have (and did) ignore in school. As did my teachers (Winter excepted). But now, seen through eyes refocused by Sketchy, these were high crimes.

"You need distraction when you do this stuff. We all do." For that, he had the added help of the old Victrola, his pipe, his Felix dolls, lunch.

And I had Tip.

"What does green sound like?" He would just . . . appear. With questions like this. Tip was forever trying to jump-start his brain to come up with ad copy, and I became his muse of choice. His favorite method was word association, and when that got tired he'd suggest the opposite.

"The opposite? Of what?"

"Of the first thing that pops into your head. Give it a whirl."

"That's nuts. Like trying to—"

"*Apply* yourself."

Right. Anyway, back to "what does green sound like?"

"I'm sorry?"

"Answer, please."

He was working on something that had to do with fertilizer at the time, that much I knew. "Green?" Well, not my thumb, that's for sure. "Hmm, I don't. Um." I soon learned to give up trying to find the "right" answer and just answer. Which was the whole point. Green sounded like . . . the woods behind our house. "Trees." In a high wind. "Trees walking."

"Oh. *Oh.* That's wonderful. Preston couldn't come up with that in a million years."

Preston Ware. Tip's boss. Head copywriter.

When he was awake. How to describe him? Tip: "He's kind of like Frankenstein's monster, only without the electricity. In a Brooks Brothers suit," and, "Pally pal, in our cigar shop, he IS the wooden Indian." Perhaps more kindly, Lars Rakoff, our dear departed co-founder, was quoted in a local news feature on Preston from 1935—clipped, framed, hung just to the left of the subject's pristine desk. He put it this way: "My partner is first and foremost a patriot, a Rotarian, an inspirational communicator, a knight." Sketch, in a private moment once at Saluzo's after work and feeling a couple thrown back, was a little more succinct: "I've always thought of him as a well-wiped asshole." I had to agree—he certainly was hygienic. Whatever the shambles of his interior life, there wasn't a hair out of place. Tip even claimed he once caught him in the men's room of the Quinnipiac Club combing his head with a salad fork after a high wind on the croquet lawn blew his comb-over to the wrong side. Square of jaw and high of forehead, he looked like an amalgam of Dag Hammarskjöld and an Easter Island monolith. He came from old money, a clan of Lake Forest Episcopalians who actually frowned on advertising as a profession, a fact that enabled Preston to think of himself, quaintly, as something of a rebel.

Company lore: Lars and Preston opened the doors of Rakoff & Ware in 1922. They met in Chicago the previous year while working at Otis & Shepherd, where they'd just landed the Wrigley's account. In a move bold for its time, they split off, fled east, and managed to take Wrigley's with them—a sort of advertising elopement. They soon brought on Spear, barely out of high school, though it would be many years before he made partner. The launch of Doublemint gum was to be their greatest triumph. Wrigley's eventually went back to O & S, under dubious circumstances, but a small slice of ad history had been carved.

"You know, Mimi notwithstanding, Lars really was a genius," said Tip. "*God,* I would have loved to meet him. That quote in the paper about Preston. Just brilliant—it took me forever to figure it out."

"Figure it out?"

"I'll show you."

We snuck into Preston's office early the next morning and he brought it down from the wall.

"Read it again. The language is too awkward—not Lars's style. That's the tip-off. This is the man who came up with '*HOLD YOUR TONGUE!*' for Buster Brown. No, when I first read it I thought, Something's going on here. I let it go for a while, and then it came to me, like when you abandon a crossword puzzle and it stews in your head for an hour or two and you come back to it and all of the answers are suddenly obvious. Only in this case it took me weeks. Look." He pointed to the citation. "The clue is 'First and foremost,' but then there's a laundry list, which is weird. And I finally realized: take the first letter of each 'attribute.' This is what he's really saying:

"Preston's a

Patriot
Rotarian
Inspirational
Communicator
Knight."

"Oh my God. That's amazing."

"And no surprise—I think he *hated* him. And figured out a way to vent it—in the press." Tip gently rehung it. "I have yet to exercise the opportunity."

Tip and Preston: could there have been two more discordant souls? Ware had long since sold his stake in the company to Mimi—first emotionally, then, much later, financially. Something about him made it hard to believe that he was ever young, it just seemed biologically impossible. He was *born* seventy. One sensed that he came to work only because he needed the ritual of leaving the house. His two children were well into their failed second marriages, and we often wondered how they were ever conceived in the first place.

"Surely not through any human contact." Tip was certain: "They must have ordered them from Rogers Peet. The only thing of Preston's that's ever been stiff is his shirt. If the world only knew: the man who wrote the selling copy underneath the immortal words *'DOUBLE YOUR PLEASURE, DOUBLE YOUR FUN!'* wouldn't know EITHER ONE if he woke up naked in a harem covered with Karo Syrup."

This was hard to dispute. Eyelids perpetually at half-mast over their ice-blue orbs, Preston showed up (impeccably dressed, yes), he wrote things, he muttered phrases, he went to lunch, he staggered back, he passed out, he woke up around five, he went home. Just in time for cocktails.

Conventional office wisdom: If you needed something from Preston, manage to get it before twelve thirty. Or wait till the next day. Before twelve thirty.

Or try to talk to Nicky.

Nicholas Rakoff, the only son of Lars and Mimi, the inheritor of the family business. I met him by accident when I was looking for Tip one afternoon with a phone message. I heard him outside the door of the conference chamber and thought he was alone, rehearsing a pitch. I bolted in. "Tip, I—"

"Shhhh."

He was at the other end of the long room, talking to someone—a distinguished man of middle age, in shirtsleeves and bow tie, hunched over. Tip murmured, gravely, "Yes, that's a better strategy, definitely." I thought at first the guy was either doubled over with grief or looking for something on the floor and couldn't bring himself to get down on his hands and knees. I could tell—he wasn't a hands-and-knees sort at all. And then I realized that he hadn't lost anything. Not yet.

"How's this?"

"That's it."

"Okay, here we go."

Cigarette clenched into lips pursed with concentration, he tilted the considerable bulk of his upper body oh so slightly to the left, and then released it. It snapped back, as if attached to a small spring, and the stick in his hands connected with something on the floor—*PAP!*—which shot perilously across the carpet in my direction, to the man's intense concern, and then—*PLUNK!*—into an overturned coffee cup a yard to the right of my wing tips. His face, his whole head, glowed with supreme satisfaction, like a jack-o-lantern.

Tip, still solemn: "Bra-*vo*. See? That new thumb technique is *flawless*." And then, brightening up a bit and finally acknowledging me, "Nicky, this is Happy—Sketch's new assistant."

Still savoring his hole-in-mug. A careless glance. Then a thought. "Great!" He approached me. Now I could finally see: he was all Golden Boy gone to seed, a Ken doll left out in the sun too long. Once molded, now molten. "We could use some new blood around here. 'Bout time!" He reached down, with effort— "Oof"—picked up the cup, rolled the ball out of it, and handed it to me. "Black. Two sugars."

"Uh—"

"Thanks, sport." And he turned back to Tip.

"Sure." It was plain from the beginning that I was nothing to him—just another admirer from the peanut gallery, ready to follow him to the next hole, to the clubhouse, to the ball washer.

I didn't think this a problem, because there was no reason to take it personally—he treated just about everyone this way because it never occurred to him not to, and yet there was something pathetically charming about it. This man was the progeny of the divine Lars, after all.

But Nicky was *not* his father. He pretty much saw the firm as a handicap to his golf game, in both senses of the word. Whenever the weather would allow he'd skip out to the Quinnippiac, with some client or other in tow "to do the back nine." And during the winter he would hole himself up in his office and putt. It wasn't that he didn't know the ad business—he did, with an accounting major's sense of directive.

He just completely hated it.

Now, while Mimi was the firm's legal owner, and it

was Nicky's responsibility to actually run the place, it would be three weeks before I met the real, driving force behind the agency. And when I did, it completely changed my mind about how an office works. On a Monday during our lunch hour, Tip and I were conducting an experiment in the second-floor hallway, he on the stairwell landing and me half a flight above, my back to his. He wanted to do a sort of blind word test. Our goal was to develop catchphrases for Krinkle's new line of flavored pretzels.

He began: "Onions!"

Me: "Tears."

"Chives!"

"Confetti." From somewhere downstairs burst a faint cry. Mimi: "*Oh Haaaaaaaammeeeeeeeee!*" I turned and looked at Tip, who either hadn't heard it or was too consumed with his analysis. I turned back. Suddenly a dark shape rounded the corner at the far end of the corridor. Moving. Fast.

Tip: "Garlic!"

"Power . . ." It skidded into the water cooler with a sloshy thud, regained its balance, and made for the other end of the hallway. Sprinting.

"Bacon!"

"Saturday?" Toward *me*.

"Brilliant! Barbecue!"

"Sunday. Tip?" Holy shit.

"Pork!"

I was frozen. Look at it!

"Oh Haaaaaaaammeeeeeeeee! Heeeeere, darling!"

"I said PORK!"

Help! "Tip!"

"What?!"

SLAM! Its head went into my stomach, then herky-jerked and rolled and—*huk!*—in a single gesture tossed me against the wall. And then was gone. It scarcely broke stride.

Tip: "Hamlet! No!" He threw himself out of its way, shielded his head with the arc of his arm. "You *lummox!* Bad!"

Papers scattered everywhere. The thing faltered and tumbled mightily down the steps, falling over itself, landed on the first floor, shook, and reared. Vanished.

I asked, trying to learn how to breathe again, "What—what was *that?*"

"That," scowled Tip, gathering up his notes, "was Mimi's husband."

Shortly before Lars's untimely death in 1955, he bestowed upon Mimi a pedigree Great Dane puppy for her sixtieth birthday and named it, yes, Hamlet. She never got the joke. And never needed to, because of what she *did* get—something she thought she'd had once, many years ago. But here was Hamlet—proof in the quivering, hirsute flesh that she was wrong. She'd *never* had this before, and now that she did . . . oh. Oh. How could she have lived without it? It wasn't that she made the dog any kind of replacement for Lars, or his keen mind, or merely his companionship. Frankly it wasn't about Lars at all. Their marriage had worked well only to the extent that He was the Money and She was the Class. What Hamlet represented, in the most concrete, literal way, was the first time that Mimi had ever experienced, ever found . . . true love.

Hamlet had full run—not just of the agency—but of Mimi's life, her soul, her nervous system. Which was incalculably nervous. The two of them together would practically vibrate in frenzied syncopation, like mixed plaids that somehow harmonized successfully, despite the laws of aesthetic cohesion.

Few who beheld it were ever able to erase the sight from their minds: Mimi on a temperate day in her pink cadillac convertible (top down, natch), cruising along Trumbull with Hamlet in the passenger seat, his monstrous head flopped over the side and leaking viscous drool like transmission fluid from a faulty, quivering hose.

Tip: "That is *not* a dog. It is Jerry Lewis, undergoing perpetual heroin withdrawal, in a dog costume."

Usually heard, sensed, and smelled before he was ever seen, Hamlet would stagger or stamp by in the hall, in frantic search of a nameless quarry, his cranium covered with dozens of Mimi's lipstick stains. The first time I encountered that, I was with Tip and he just couldn't help himself: "Check between his legs. Go ahead. You'll find a whole *rash* of them."

By the second week, I'd earned enough of Sketch's trust to start penciling some hand lettering for him to ink. He was a master of what's called display type, usually elaborate script, which was used for the headlines and sub-heads. As a rule he relied on as little machine typesetting as possible, only for the large blocks of sales copy. This was an aesthetic decision; but because he was as fast at it as he was brilliant, it also helped keep the bills down. And that, I soon learned, was what it was all about. I had to precisely record exactly how much time I spent on each job and for whom, so the billable hours were charged to the right client for the right amount. I'd never had to literally account for my time this way in my life and at first it was oppressive and draconian. I considered myself an organized person, but this crossed a line. As long as I got the job done, on time, what the hell did it matter? There were also times when for reasons of technical complication I was working on two jobs at once. What to do then?

"Bill 'em both the same."

"Gotcha."

This, when I thought about it, was as ingenious as it was unethical, and I came to learn that most ad agencies do it. And nearly all law firms.

However, once I got used to meticulously chronicling my hours and who was to pay for them and it became second nature, I began to rely on it as a comfort. It was an imposed diary, recorded evidence of my life on Earth that I otherwise wouldn't have created. I kept personal copies of all of my time sheets out of a fevered nostalgia, the way I still had all my valentines from fourth grade. See? I was *needed.*

It wouldn't be long before I was summoned to my first client meeting. Sketch thought it was time I met one of the people I was really working for. We had the week's new potato chip ads to show and I'd done all the coupons myself. I was terrified, convinced that I'd be recognized as the feeble neophyte I was.

"Happy, Mr. Stankey."

A hand was extended. Or was it a baseball glove molded out of human skin?

"Pleased ta meetcha, kid. I'm Dick."

Just one of the many attributes of Dick Stankey, the client representative for Krinkle Kutt, was there was no need to waste time coming up with something funny to call him behind his back. Even Tip didn't bother. "I just use his real name and try to keep a straight face. How do you improve on perfection? *Dickens* couldn't have come up with better: 'Let's see, what do I call a three-hundred-pound potato chip salesman who's scarcely five feet two, sweats like a roasting ham hock, plays the theme to *Your Show of Shows* on the ukulele, and once got stuck in a diner booth during a fire alarm?'" All true. But what a good sport—when it came to making fun of him, he'd beat you to it. He was the first flesh-real jolly fat person I'd ever met, smiling even when he wasn't smiling, his eyes forced into delighted squints by the physics of face flab. A bag of Krinkles forever grafted onto one of his mitts, he devoted himself to enjoying his company's product in full view of humanity and did so with unashamed abandon in his office, his car, at our drawing tables, before and after lunch. Unfortunately, he also chewed tobacco at the same time. How he negotiated these two digestive actions (which I held to be at alarmingly violent cross-purposes) I could not know. I tried not to think about it, but did. A lot.

On top of all of that, he had man-bosoms. Tip was enthralled. "Talk about he-lights! You just know Meem's bitty titties lie awake at night, desperately longing to somehow usurp through osmosis the heft and shape of Stankey's." Mimi was flat as a mesa. "And they shall be forever wanting."

Even if he hadn't had such an agreeable personality I would have liked Dick Stankey anyway because he regarded Sketch with something like worship and genuinely greeted each new ad with the infectious enthusiasm of a mongoloid child grabbing a nice bright red balloon.

"That's amazing! Oooooooooh! Ooh! Oh!"

And boy, was he right. Sketch didn't so much draw newspaper ads as he created magic worlds to step into that just happened to be populated with potato chips and pretzels. I came to understand that he took as his inspiration the Sunday comics pages he'd read as a child, back when they truly were an art form. Gasoline Alley, The Kinder Kids, Polly and Her Pals, Skippy, and of course Little Nemo—all of them were made with a virtuosic care and skill that wouldn't survive to the 1940s. And they were regarded by most of the public as fishwrap. Yes, some of them survived and were reprinted, but many were not, and what Sketch was doing—at least for himself as much as for Krinkle Kutt—was keeping their spirit alive. I'm sure Mimi never understood that; but Dick did, and this, I have since learned, is the key to every single interesting piece of graphic design that you have ever seen. Winter explained to us in graphic design class once, during a critique on corporate trademarks, his face a mask of righteous accusation. But we were too naive to grasp it:

> *Kiddies, what makes good design is*
> *good clients. It's as simple as that.*
> *Look at CBS—the eye. Genius. But*
> *Frank Stanton, the head of the net-*
> *work, deserves as much credit as Bill*
> *Golden, who actually designed it. If*
> *the sumvabitch paying the bills isn't*
> *on your bus, you ain't going any-*
> *where. But if he really lets you drive,*
> *you can gun it to the moon.*

Dick Stankey gave Sketch the keys, went to the rear of the coach, sat back with a delighted grin, and— buffeted by the roar of the engine—gleefully crunched.

And spat. To the moon.

"When did Sketch make partner?" I don't know why I asked it.

Tip was on his second scotch at Mory's. A Friday lunch. "That's a funny story, actually. Classic Mimi. I once got it out of Preston at a breakfast meeting. You know," he leaned in, "here's the thing: the Meems occasionally betrays moments of lucidity that are positively frightening. Sketch was last to make partner and yet his name is ahead of the other two. Now, why do you suppose, that is?"

"I dunno. Because he has the most talent?"

"Oh, right. As if that would cross what's left of her mind in a million years. No, here it is: Mimi said she wanted Spear's name first, and I quote: 'So it sounds like we have a point,' unquote. Now, as atomically idiotic as that may seem, you have to admit: the ring of 'Spear, Rakoff and Ware' just somehow *works*. Right? Scary."

And we took that particular ball and ran with it, waging an informal, open-ended contest to see who could mangle our firm's good name in the most supreme fashion. It started the morning Tip picked up a call from the main desk when Preechy was out on an errand and no one else was within earshot (except me, of course). He intoned, in a dead-on imitation of her:

"Dear, Slack Off Your Cares. May I help you?"

Which led to my rough sketch for the New Haven Hospital Annex brochure that I sent to Tip via interoffice dispatch, with the headline: "Severe Lacking of Care."

It all became about context. A discreet note on the kitchen pantry's bulletin board: "Sneer, Crack-up and Stare. How may I deflect you?"

From there, anything went. Bored, I'd dial Tip in the middle of the afternoon: "Hello, I'm calling from Smear Lacquer on Chair."

Pasted over a Food Clown circular, shoved into my mail slot: "We're . . . hacking up pears!"

My proposed Bubble-Soap Shampoo campaign slogan: "Rear back from her hair!"

A Sunbeam Bakery meeting's minutes subject heading: "Mere rack of eclairs."

On an internal memo for Preston's seventieth birthday: "Queer attack over there!"

A business card for Closter's Driving School, shoved under the door, the title crossed out and replaced with: "Veer, back up and dare!"

But I got the best one, as Preston passed me and Tip in the hall one day, doing what Tip called the Muffle Shuffle—eyes clenched and lips moving wordlessly as he staggered along, groping for the right word. And it was so obvious. I stage-whispered into Tip's ear:

"Sheer, wracking despair."

And just then he happened to stick his head into Nicky's office, and asked, with desperate, laconic impatience: "Is it lunchtime yet?"

It was nine thirty.

• • •

And then came that day of days, which yielded the first ad I ever designed entirely by myself. June 20th, a Tuesday afternoon, close to three. Sketchy was out on a printing-press check and Miss Preech forwarded the call to me.

"Hello?"

Of course, I've thought about that day a lot. Because of what eventually happened. But I've never felt it could have gone any differently—if Sketch hadn't been away from the office, say, or if the call came when I was out at lunch. That wouldn't have changed anything. I'm really no great believer in "destiny," and yet I know this job would have found its way to me, regardless of the circumstances. It was inevitable.

"I'd like to place an ad in the *Register*." A man's voice, deep. "They told me to contact your firm." We were the *New Haven Register*'s largest subcontractor for advertising. Well, okay, the only one. They were always lobbing little jobs at us—the ones their staff (of two) didn't have time for.

"Right." I reached for a job ticket and a fresh piece of carbon paper. "What kind of ad?"

"We need to recruit people for an experiment."

"I see. What do you want it to say?"

He explained. For what seemed like half an hour.

This was a lot of information. Me: "Hmmm. Is it a full page?"

"Oh, heavens no. We couldn't afford that. An eighth of a page, to run daily. That's what we can afford."

An eighth of a page. Insane. "Wow. That won't be easy."

"Can you make it fit?"

Can I make it fit? Sigh.

That is a question that begs a brief typographic digression (sorry).

Typography is truly the invisible art of the last one hundred years, even though it is in plain sight, everywhere. Most graphic design students learn this right away, but we also discover just as quickly that we're in the vast minority. It all becomes distressingly clear once we leave the rarified halls of learning, enter the steaming ranks of the working learned, and show them classic typefaces, correct letter spacing, proper line leading, and exacting proportions.

And they don't give a damn.

"I can't read it."

"Make it bigger."

"Make it smaller."

"It's too precious."

"It's too bold."

"It's too plain."

"It all has to go on one page. Make it sing!"

"Cut some of the copy? You're joking."

To them, it's just words, but to us, to graphic designers, it's *type*. We've learned to look at it a whole other way. Notice I said "look" instead of "read." Once again, Form and Content take center field – will they strangle each other? Will they get married? Will they at least hold hands?

This is the eternal typographic conundrum. What most people don't understand is that typography is the use of language that in itself is its own language –

one that can take a lifetime to learn and perfect, and that few ever do. Put simply: The Content is, of course, what the words say, the Form is what they look like. But alas, it's rarely as clear cut as that. Before the advent of what was called Commercial Art this was less of an issue than it is now, but as we find ourselves thick into the age of the visual dispatch, there is no turning back. It's not just about what you're saying anymore, it's how you're saying it. In the wrong hands, mixed messages abound. Suppose you have something important to convey to a loved one:

I hate you.

This misrepresents your sentiment. As opposed to:

I hate you.

Right? And yet, this same design solution would not be wanted in a report from your personal physician:

The test results are in:

You have inoperable cancer!!

Now let's try solicitation, as we constantly apply it in the ad trade. This can get tricky. Like so:

PLEASE TOUCH ME.

Whoops! Creepy, creepy. I don't think so. Which brings us back to:

Please touch me.

You see? Endless possibilities. And pitfalls.

Now, let's apply this to practical use, namely to the newspaper advertisement I was commissioned to design in the summer of 1961. The client placed the order by phone, which can complicate the choosing of typefaces, but luckily in this case that was one aspect of the job about which — surprise! — he couldn't have cared less. Brief recap:

"Hello. I'd like to place an advertisement in the *Register*, please."

"Yessir. What kind of ad?"

"It's for the Yale Department of Psychology. We're conducting an experiment and we'd like to solicit volunteers from the community."

"I see. What do you want the ad to say?"

He went on. And on. Finally:

"Gee. That's a lot of information. Is this a full page?"

"Oh, heavens no. We couldn't afford that. We checked the rates — this would be less than a quarter page. An eighth, I believe."

Impossible. Are you out of your goddamn mind? You're not supposed to be, Mr. Yale Psychology Department. "Less than a quarter page, with all this copy? Can you cut any of it?"

"Well, no."

Did he have any idea what he was asking? Of course not. They never do. "Right. Uh, this will be a little tricky. Let me spec this out. I could show it to you tomorrow afternoon."

"That . . . won't be necessary. Just run it. Today if you can. I'm sure it will be fine."

"Really?" Now *that* was odd. They're usually like vultures.

"Yes, just make all the information as big as possible."

As I eventually learned, over time, they all say that. ALL OF THEM.

"Okay, will do."

"Thanks."

So, here is the final ad, as it ran, with several notations:

PUBLIC ANNOUNCEMENT

WE WILL PAY YOU $4.00 FOR ONE HOUR OF YOUR TIME.

Persons needed for a study of memory.

- We will pay 500 New Haven men to help us complete a scientific study of memory and learning. The study is being done at Yale University.
- Each person who participates will be paid $4.00 (plus 50¢ carfare) for approximately 1 hour's time. We need you for only 1 hour. There are no further obligations. You may choose the time you would like to come (evenings, weekdays, or weekends).

NO SPECIAL TRAINING, EDUCATION, OR EXPERIENCE IS NEEDED. WE WANT:

Factory Workers	Businessmen	Construction Workers
City Employees	Clerks	Salespeople
Laborers	Professional People	White-collar Workers
Barbers	Telephone Workers	Others

ALL PERSONS MUST BE BETWEEN THE AGES OF 20 AND 50. HIGH SCHOOL AND COLLEGE STUDENTS CANNOT BE USED.

- If you meet these qualifications, fill out the coupon below and mail it now to Professor Stanley Milgram, Department of Psychology, Yale University, New Haven. You will be notified later of the specific time and place of the study. We reserve the right to decline any application.
- You will be paid $4.00 (plus 50¢ carfare) as soon as you arrive at the laboratory.

TO: PROF. STANLEY MILGRAM, DEPARTMENT OF PSYCHOLOGY, YALE UNIVERSITY, NEW HAVEN, CONN.

I want to take part in this study of memory and learning. I am between the ages of 20 and 50. I will be paid $4.00 (plus 50¢ carfare) if I participate.

NAME (PLEASE PRINT) ....

ADDRESS ....

TELEPHONE NO. ....BEST TIME TO CALL ....

AGE ....OCCUPATION ....

I CAN COME: WEEKDAYS ....EVENINGS ....WEEKENDS ....

First, note that there are no less than eleven different kinds of information to be considered, in a space that is 3 3/4 inches wide x 6 inches tall. Even so, only three typeface "families" are used (Trade Gothic, Bodoni, and Baskerville), each with its own set of variations to provide enough typographical "color" without appearing busy or jammed. In order to maintain proper proportions, some of the type must be reduced to 7 points, widely regarded as the absolute minimal for legibility (a theory with which those over fifty years of age may strenuously disagree).

1. This must be listed first, for legal reasons, but is by no means the most important piece of information. I used 9-point Trade Gothic Condensed, a classic sans-serif typeface used primarily in tabloid newspaper headlines that can easily withstand this kind of reduction and still look important, especially in all capital letters.

2. All caps again, but this time in a classic 12-point Bodoni medium weight, which commands center of attention – it is designed to be the first thing you see. After they finally saw the ad, it took some convincing for Yale to accept that this is the reason people would respond, as opposed to any sense of "civic duty" to further the cause of "science." It is offset by two .5-point lines, or "rules," for emphasis.

3. Back to Trade Gothic, in a lighter weight and caps/lowercase. This should be the second line you see/read.

4. The first block of what we call "body copy," in 7-point Baskerville, a popular text face for English literature. The dots, or "bullets," prioritize the two distinct groups of information within. Note that the amount of compensation to the solicitee is mentioned four times throughout the ad. This was their idea, not mine.

5, 6. By grouping this list into three columns, I not only saved space, I made it easier for the eye to process. A solid paragraph with the titles offset by commas would be far more taxing.

7, 8. The second block of body copy is set off by a headline in all-caps Baskerville (the only one). It is noticeably wider than the first block (4), both to economize space and to make it distinct.

9, 10. Coupons, it must be said, are a burden for both the designer and the typesetter, but at least in this case it serves to "anchor" the entire composition. The border is a series of short straight lines, indicating detachment, while the "blanks" to be filled in are denoted by dots. The professor's name and position, as it were, are italicized to impart a sense of urgency on the part of the reader. Ideally, two lines should be allocated for the address, but space limitations made this impossible.

11. If you look closely you'll see one dot less after the word "Weekends." This provides a subtle but undeniable message: weekdays and evenings are preferred.

The ad had been running every day now for three weeks, and no order to stop it—by far the longest life of anything I'd worked on. Shamelessly, I'd hunt it down each morning in the *Register* like a parent looking for his child on the crowded stage of a kindergarten play. Where was it? Next to the Red Sox scores? Above the movie listings? Below Dear Abby? No . . . there it is, by the horoscopes! Yoo-hoo! Daaaarling!

I'd clip its entire host page, fold it in fours, and add it to the growing stack next to my tool tray. In case I needed them for reference, to study how it looked in the context of the other ads next to it. At least that's what I told myself.

Ridiculous. It was just a dumb solicitation, a type-heavy, glorified want ad. Forget it. Let it go.

And for a while, I did.

• • •

"So, what you're telling me is, you lost my rhinoceros head. Is that what you're telling me?"

By the beginning of July things were going pretty well, so I guess it was inevitable: Himillsy Dodd chose then to come back into my life. In her own special way.

"You said importing it through you guys would be no problem. That's a three-hundred-dollar rhinoceros head, pal. They don't grow on *trees.*"

Now, some of you might be wondering why I haven't mentioned her before. There are many reasons, but for those who are unfamiliar—she takes over whenever she's involved. Or, as she once put it (muttered in sotted distaste at a Phi Delt mixer back at school): *"I am the corpse at every wedding, I am the bride at every funeral."* And this was to be no exception.

"Three centuries, buddy. Cough him up."

We'd met my freshman year at State. She was a junior. I was captivated. And she was, too—at least that's what she led me to believe. Together we went through an art school bootcamp the likes of which neither of us expected, and we came out of it booted—me out of every preconception about art and design that I ever had, and she from sanity (and the school) altogether. Our parting was not an easy or coherent one, chiefly because of what I'd perceived, over the phone, to be her total nervous breakdown. Which I admit I played a part in, however unwittingly. For Himillsy, living dangerously was the only way to live. And me, I'm practically a crossing guard. More than once I'd spoiled her fun, rescuing her from something she didn't want to be saved from. And who is ever forgiven for that? I was her unwanted conscience, the Jiminy Cricket to her Pinocchio, forever doing her good turns. For that alone I suppose she had every right to hate me.

Then nothing, no contact for the next three years. But she was never far from my thoughts, from the moment of our first meeting.

"What do you mean, 'We know where it is'? I know what that means: On Earth. Somewhere between here and the tiny Republic of Togo. *Jesus.*"

Here's what I did know, long before I ever came to Connecticut: Himillsy had grown up just twenty minutes away, in Guilford, and her family still lived there (they were listed). I'd mused that with any luck she might even be still living with them. And I had an eye on getting in touch once I got my feet on the ground, as it were. Once I got the nerve.

And now the nerve had gotten *me.*

"Enough of you. Where's your supervis—" She turned, and finally saw me, standing in the checkout line of the campus Art Depot, clutching six jars of fluorescent egg tempera to my chest on a summer Saturday afternoon. Neither of us could believe it. Our eyes met, vaporizing three years in three seconds. "Oh. My. God." Her face hadn't changed—Betty Boop meets cute with the Dragon Lady. Ditto her figure, size zero in a sleeveless linen cocktail dress the color of dried mustard. A tiara of Ray-Bans perched over her forehead. Mascara applied with a trowel and a quivering hand.

"Uh—" I replied, a reflex.

"Since *when*," she started, staggering toward me, her eyes dark with horrified concern, "have you been painting with *fluorescent* colors?"

"Since *when*," I countered, leaving the queue, "do you have a rhinoceros head?"

"I *don't* have it. Haven't you been paying attention? The simpletons in charge of this salvage sale have lost it." She clicked her tongue in disgust. "Can you imagine? It's the size of a large dwarf and weighs two hundred pounds. It's like losing the front end of a DeSoto."

The manager eased toward her, cautiously. "Ma'am, I . . . I keep telling you, it's not lost. It's being held in Customs."

Oh, I thought, you poor man. You have no idea who or what you're dealing with.

"*Cus*toms? What, are they waiting for the *rest* of it to show up?"

"Miss Dodd," I said, calmly, "science has shown us that the severed rhinoceros head is the breeding ground of choice for the notorious and deadly tsetse fly. One nostril alone could comfortably house an entire colony. Surely this would be of grave concern to our government."

The manager gaped at me, desperate with gratitude for any explanation, however untenable. "Yes! That's it exactly."

She shouldered her slate Chanel purse and smoothed her ebony Lulu helmet of hair. "You were always like that," she sneered at me. "Always."

"What, right?"

"No. *Infuriating.*" Her scowl melted into a sly grin and she made for the door, pausing to address the manager. "I'll be back in a week and that head had better be here. Or I'll have yours." And, jerking *her* lovely head in my direction, out she went.

I hastily abandoned the paint jars to the nearest shelf and followed. As I did in the old days.

My whole body was smiling. Himillsy, you're here.

You're really here.

• • •

The proprietors of Pepe's Pizza on Wooster Street boldly claim that they, and only they, originated this most ubiquitous of delectations here in the United States, and more specifically, in New Haven. Which may or may not be true, but this much is indisputable: they are not open for lunch. Dinner only, the bastards.

So Himillsy suggested (proclaimed, actually) that we go to Modern Apizza (pronounce "Abeetz"), their biggest rival in town for the crust crown. They start serving at noon.

"Besides, it's better," she said, gunning the engine of her Corvair, "the sauce has more tang. Everyone's afraid to say it." The "but not me" went unsaid. It always did.

I was still in a kind of shock—were I to wake up in my bed in the next second, Himillsy gone like a smoke ring, I would not have been surprised.

But there she sat, as real as three years ago when we used to cruise down College Avenue: head scarcely clearing the dashboard, lacquered ebony fingernails orbiting the stick shift, the world behind her racing past, ever trying to keep up.

God, Hims. If there's a word for how much I've missed you, it's not in my vocabulary.

"Stop staring at me. I'm not the Hottentot Venus."

"Sorry. It's just that—"

"And what happened to your neon paint? Lose your nerve?"

"I put it on hold. Something came up."

"Did it. And that would be . . . ?"

"The human equivalent."

She chuckled dryly, pulled over onto State and into a spot across the street from the restaurant. After she turned the engine off, she hesitated, chortling: "*In*human, darling."

She didn't bother with the menu. "We'll have a large red, light on the motz, quarters: sausage, mushrooms, onions, pepperoni. Extra sauce. And two Rocks."

We got the last booth before the rush. Dean Martin oozed "That's Amore" over the loudspeakers. The impasto paintings of the Ponte Vecchio and the Leaning Tower of Pisa were fifth-rate, but the perfume of broiled garlic and simmering San Marzano tomatoes wafting from the ovens was perfection. A waitress in a red-and-white–checkered gingham number that matched the tablecloths planted the beers in front of us.

Himillsy shook out a Lucky Strike and returned her sunglasses to their upright position. "Did you ever think about brains?"

"What?"

"I'm in a brain phase. Brains are *just* amazing. I'm crazy for them. I've been making scads of brains, whole regiments, out of Plasticine."

"Brains."

"In all sizes. And colors."

"Except fluorescent."

"Especially NOT fluorescent." She flicked open her Reddy Kilowatt Zippo and sparked her cigarette. "Too much to bear. But you really ought to consider brains. Dangerously overlooked. You're missing out, trust me."

"How so?"

"Well, first of all," she was really fired up now, a martinet on a mission: "did you know that we only use ten percent of our brains? It's totally amazing. One. Tenth. The rest is pure mystery."

We hadn't seen each other for a third of a decade. Why were we talking about *this*? "And just how was that proven, exactly?"

"Easily. Look at all of human history."

"You'll have to do better than that."

"Why? Mankind sure hasn't. We're a bunch of lunkheads! I mean really, just look at the past ten years—Styrofoam, McCarthy, Disneyland, the Korean War, Liberace, frozen spaghetti. Come *on*. I seriously doubt we use even ten percent, most of the time. It's the geniuses that can tap into the rest—*that's* what's interesting. I've been doing brain exercises."

"Have you now."

"Don't laugh. I'm very serious."

Should I say it? "Actually . . . it's bunk."

It was as if I'd just spilled the beans on Santa Claus to a five-year-old. "What is?"

"The ten percent thing. We learned it in second-year Psych. There's still a lot they don't know, for sure, but it's a common misconception, since the turn of the century. When they were finally able to study it with any accuracy."

She was not liking this. Not one bit.

Might as well continue. "See, the fact is that only ten percent of your brain cells are *neurons*, the key cells used in learning. And of those, only ten percent of your neurons can fire at any given time, or else your head would explode. When someone has a seizure, that's what's happening."

I could practically see the steam shoot out of her ears. Instead, smoke issued in mighty plumes from her nose—she the dragging dragon.

"It's not fair to be actually *informed* on the subject," she hissed, crushing out her smoke for emphasis. "You have no manners."

"Well, I'm—"

"ANYway, brains are my thing right now and that's that." She threw back a healthy slug of brew. "I think they're beautiful. I've changed the name of our cat to Bulbous Medulla. He's having none of it, but tough titty, kitty." Then: "All right, smartyboots. So what are you doing here?"

"Having lunch, I hope."

"Cretin." She fired off two matches together from the side of a Modern's tinderbox, lit up, inhaled. "To what does the godforsaken necropolis of New Haven owe your divine intervention?"

"Can't you guess? I got a job. At that advertising

agency. Spear, Rakoff and Ware, on Trumbull Street."

She propelled another cloud to the ceiling and waited for me to continue.

"Remember?" I said, "Jeez, that whole thing, back at school, with Winter's assignment and the Wrigley's wrapper? I had to find out who designed it? Which led me to—"

"You got a *job*? *Here*?"

As if she hadn't understood a thing I just told her. Could she have forgotten? It wasn't that long ago, was it? "It's an advertising firm. Don't you remember?"

"As a matter of fact, I don't." Another puff. "I can't remember the last time I puked, either."

So much for talking about the past. Here, in closer captivity, I could see that she had indeed aged. Worry lines began their slight yet unstoppable journey outward from her tired eyes. But it was more than just the years. Something about her was different. Something profound had happened to her. Not anything good.

"I never pegged you for the advertising type," she remarked, not a little condescendingly.

"Well, what type *did* you—"

"Careful," said the waitress, "it's hot."

The pie was presented in what appeared to be an aluminum cookie sheet, bubbling like lava. It was round, but sliced into small squares.

When I remarked on this, Himillsy explained: "I figured it out when I was little—they cut it this way so you'll eat more of it."

"And how does that work?"

"Geometry. It's like writing an epic novel in little one-page chapters. Much easier to digest. Insidious."

The only thing insidious about it was that I couldn't get enough of it. Hims didn't so much eat the pizza as inhale it, all the while grunting from the pain. "If it doesn't burn off the roof of your mouth you're just not enjoying it."

I had to agree.

Not ten minutes later, with the pan picked clean, we ordered another round of suds.

"You settled here by yourself?" she asked.

"Yes."

"What, still haven't found the right girl?" It was more sinister accusation than question. Hims and I had never been romantic. Not even hinted at, though at the time I told myself I would have liked that. But not now, and she knew why. I think she always did. Which was why she was asking. Oh, Hims, there's not a scab you won't pick at, is there?

"Apparently not," I said curtly, answering both our questions. "And you, what have you been up to, besides brains? How's Garnett?" (Her boyfriend from college.)

She used the dying embers of her cigarette to inflame a fresh one. "Garnett? God, who knows, who cares?"

You did, at the time. "I don't if you don't."

"I don't."

"Right." I couldn't help myself—memories bubbled to the surface like hungry goldfish. "God, do you remember that crazy Christmas party you two gave that time? You got so loaded you–"

"No." Not as in "I don't remember." As in "that's gone now." The whites in her eyes: ice.

"Sorry." Subject change needed. "So what's all this about a rhinoceros head?" Knowing her, plans to turn it into a kinetic sculpture were not out of the question.

"What?" She glared at me, accusing. "That's personal."

"Sorry."

"Really, can't a simple country girl purchase one little rhinoceros head without it becoming a federal case? Is that what we're paying our taxes for? You can bet this never happened to Margaret Mead. Oh, you can bet *that.*"

Simple. If there is anything you definitely are not, Hims, my kaleidoscopic goddess, it's simple.

"Are you listening to me?"

"Perpetually."

"Liar."

"Oh, wrong." Tell her: "You have no idea. I listen to you all the time. I always did." Admit it: "Do you know what I used to do? I used to build you in my head. So I could still talk to you. I still do."

"What?" she asked, incredulous. "WHY on earth would you do that?"

"Because you left."

Oh no. Wrong thing to say and the wrong way to say it. Wrong wrong wrong. Dammit. It was as if I'd belted her with a baseball bat. "Look, I'm sorry, I—"

"Don't." She turned to the window, lowered her sunglasses, fumbled with her cig. "Just. Don't."

The waitress brought fresh bottles and cleared the table.

A dreadful limbo. Himillsy took a sip, slowly brought us out of it. "I went through . . . a rough patch. I'm sure I don't have to tell you. And I wouldn't anyway. Too boring. Too Zelda Fitzgerald."

"But, you *are* through it." I was half asking, half asserting.

"So they tell me."

"They."

"That's . . . enough for now." She said quietly, stubbing out the butt and waving for the check, "I've got this." She laid down a ten spot on the bill, grateful for the diversion, shoving it to the edge of the table. Another slug from the bottle. That taken care of, she suddenly brightened, changing moods like a new pair of culottes. "Hey, it's a whole new world, now, right? It's the 1960s, for Chrissakes! For the first time in history there's someone in the White House I'd actually like to blow."

"You want to *blow* Jackie?"

Furious giggling. Fully herself again. "You're *obscene*." Standing, gathering her keys, "So, where are you hanging your hat? I'll drop you."

"What, no Skellar?" Back at school, especially on a Saturday afternoon, pizza would have been just the beginning—on to the Teke Sunset Luau, on to the Tri-

Delt Try-more, on to Acacia's Midnight Mixer, on to the Skeller, onto the floor.

"Not today, sport."

"Oh. Cleaned up your act?"

"How dare you? My act was always *immaculate*. I was practically a nun."

"None the *wiser*."

"Bastard."

I told her the address and cross street and in five minutes we slowed to a stop at my apartment house.

"Thanks for lunch. Can I—?" I didn't want it to end. I wanted everything. I wanted her and Tip to meet. They would really get a kick out of each other. "It's . . . been so great to see you, after all this time."

She bristled, not comfortable.

"Can I see you again soon?"

A smirk. "Not if I see you first."

"Really. I mean it."

"I'm *teasing*," she purred, putting it in first. "Give me a call next week. We'll set something up."

I got out of the car and leaned back into the window. "So . . ."

"So what?"

So much I wanted to say, how I'd missed her dreadfully, that the idea we could be friends again jumpstarted my heart. But I couldn't—she'd only make fun. Turn anything into a joke so you don't have to face it. But that was okay. Because now I'd never have to miss her again. I was asking for it, I didn't care, wanted it with greedy desperation: "So, if I'm not the advertising type, what type *did* you have me pegged for?"

She lowered her eyelids, considered it, then, "Oh, you know. The decorative, serif type."

• • •

Almost three weeks later, a Thursday afternoon. In the past twenty-one days I had tried to call Himillsy four times—the first two it was busy, the second two no one was home. Then things got really crazy at work. I'd meant to stay on it, set up a dinner date. I really had.

Ring, ring.

"Art department."

"Hi, dear."

Mom. I didn't encourage it, but it was no secret she positively luxuriated in confirming, weekly, my gainful employment. What mother didn't, I supposed. And yes, I didn't entirely mind the confirmation myself. We ran through all the usual: When was I coming home, it's been too long, Aunt Sophie is trying to run her life, Dad's working too hard, the car port needs reshingling, the Riordans next door got a new Ford when they hadn't even paid for the last one. And then.

"Honey . . . "

Oh. Something's wrong. A sad switch had been thrown in her. Anyone's guess: One of the dogs was sick. The Symphony Ladies had blackballed her. Something. "What. What is it?"

"That's such a shame about your friend, the girl."

What? "Girl? What girl?"

"The one who sent you the present that time." Present? What did she think she was saying? "From Connecticut. Remember that Christmas?" No. Himillsy? How could she be talking about Himillsy? "I'm pretty sure it's the same girl. The name is so memorable. Oh, hon, there was a story about it in your paper."

My paper. The minute my parents heard that my first ad was running in the *Register*, Mom got a subscription. Which I thought was a little excessive—local news far from their locality. But she read it compulsively, as if it would somehow tell her what was going on in my life. Good God, maybe it did. "Did you see it?"

"Mom, see *what*?"

"Honey . . . she's gone. She's . . ."

Someone threw a shotput into my stomach . . .

"It was a traffic accident."

. . . growing into a bowling ball. I choked out the words: "A traffic accident?"

"She couldn't get out of her car."

"Who, who are we talking about?"

"That girl. Him---Himsey?"

No. "Himillsy?" Impossible.

"That's it. Himillsy. I always remembered the name—"

"It can't . . . "

"Didn't you know? Oh, I'm *sorry*, dear."

She's confused. She got the story wrong. She was always doing this, mangling messages—the plots of movies, thirdhand accounts of domestic disputes from relatives, recipe measurements, stories about me as a child. She was selectively allergic to details. That's what this was. "What are you saying? What happened?"

"It was in the paper. Last Sunday. Wait, I saved it." She left the phone, returned. She read.

Time stopped.

"Hello? Honey?"

I had yet to see it. Until I did I told myself there was hope. I would not believe it until I saw it, typeset, off-set printed onto newsprint. Kerned properly. Eight-point Century Schoolbook on 10 points leading. Until I saw this I would, not, believe it.

"I'm sorry, dear."

So unacceptable was not just the thing itself, but that I was hearing it from my mother. That was *wrong*. An intrusion. This was private. She had no right. They'd never met, there was no connection between them, ever.

Except *me*.

Me: "I have. I have to go now. I need to find the story in the paper. I need to find it. Find it. I need, to read it." I was babbling, a walleyed wretch walking away, without a scratch, from a head-on collision that should have killed me. "See it."

She didn't want to hang up, not while her child was like this. I made an effort to restore my voice to normal and said some other things to her, anything to get off the phone. I'M FINE, REALLY. I HAVE TO GO NOW. THERE'S SOMEONE IN MY OFFICE. OKAY THEN. RIGHT. I HAVE A MEETING. YES, I'M SURE. WE'LL TALK SOON. THANKS. LOVE YOU, TOO.

At some point she acquiesced. Or I just hung up. (No, I didn't.) And then I went to the Records Room, our file copies of the paper. To see. How, how on earth had I missed it? Answer, of course: Because it was probably on the Obits page, which Mom always read in our local paper at the breakfast table with uncharacteristic fascination. I hated the Obits page. Its form was completely divorced from its content—there was no compassion. If I had my way, the first thing I'd do is make the whole page black for starters, with white type. I mean, how hard is *that* to figure out? It only— oh. Oh God.

AREA WOMAN, 25, FOUND DEAD

Carbon Monoxide Poisoning Suspected.

GUILFORD. — The body of a twenty-five-year-old female identified as Himillsy Dodd, daughter of Wesley and Sandra Dodd, was discovered unconscious at the wheel of her 1960 Corvair convertible in the garage of her parents' home at 302 Cobblefield Lane Friday evening. Officials believe she started the engine at approximately six o'clock and was overcome by fumes before she could raise the garage's door. Attempts to revive her proved unsuccessful. Miss Dodd was pronounced dead at New Haven Hospital at 8:41 pm. Services are to be held at Christ Episcopal Church, 11 am. Saturday.

No. No no no no no. A traffic accident. Jesus. She *did* get the story wrong.

Just not wrong enough.

This was impossible. There was no sign, none. I would have picked it up, I would have, I would have. I replayed our lunch together, over and over. There was melancholy, yes, but that was standard for her. She promised she would see me again. You don't say you're going to see someone again soon, you don't *promise* it, and then do this. It's not right it's not right.

Not if I see you first.

The floor. It was slowly rising, taking up my legs, my body, my arms, my head. My useless brain. Take me up. Take it all. My unused ten percent.

• • •

I'd never been to a funeral before. Well, once. For Grandma, the only living grandparent I'd ever known—Dad's mom, widowed for decades—a sweet and generous woman who looked like an older version of Dad in a wig. Died in her sleep at eighty-five. I was fourteen. The service was, naturally, a serious, head-bowed affair; but it wasn't as if everyone was wailing like banshees. The talk was a veritable orgy of reassurance. *She lived a good, long life. What a wonderful family she left. Gone to her reward. She's with Iden again, God bless. Do you have a map to the reception?* During the homily, my peripheral vision caught Dad's eyes discreetly leaking, his hands slowly wrestling each other to a draw. I stared straight ahead at the cross of lilies. Afterward, at the Young Republican's Club, there was punch and cookies. And stingers.

But I suspected this funeral, in Guilford, was going to be something else entirely. I had no idea.

After a short struggle with myself over whether or not to go, I then gave in: I just had to. It was my last chance to . . . to what? See her? No. Too late. But—and I know how this sounds—it would be . . . Oh God . . . the last thing we'd ever do together.

• • •

On Saturday morning I stepped with no little uncertainty from the bus onto the sidewalk adjoining the Guilford green, a large expanse of lawn and trees which could have been a life-size version of a New England town for a Lionel train set. A wilting August day, already 85 in the shade, and my navy wool suit clung to me like moss. I took a deep lungful of the wet velvet air, as the cicadas in the massive corridors of elms swelled it thick with their modulated, invisible electricity.

And then I noticed the cars. Lincolns, Cadillacs, Studebakers, a Packard, a Mercury, a smart little MGA, a Corvette convertible. All lining the green and dotted with white mums, like ivory buttons on blazer sleeves. A sick feeling bloomed in me. This is real. This is really happening. These cars are here and they have flowers taped onto them because Himillsy is dead. I gulped another heavy breath, caught my balance.

Formally dressed couples struggled out of identical Ford woody station wagons, slowly, from either the weight of the occasion or the heat or both. Sunglasses and ebony wing tips, black linen shifts, pillbox hats with veils, elbow gloves, obsidian patent leather purses the size and shape of bricks suspended from spaghetti straps. I joined their wordless caravan, trying to convince myself I belonged among them. Absurd. The cozy Grover's Corners perfection of the buildings surrounding the park—Dowden's Drugstore, Murphy's Hardware, Noah's Diner—made me want to stop and throw rocks at them. It wasn't right for the world to go about its business.

Christ Episcopal Church, a granite monolith, stood out in defiance against the pristine clapboard rectitude of its neighbors. Twin doors the color of fresh blood flanked its stony facade, a block carved with the date 1838. Inside, it was marginally cooler, with four ceiling fans going like jet propellers as the sunlight ricocheted off the custard stucco walls and Pachelbel's endless *Canon* oozed in and out of the organ pipes mounted to the left of the lectern. The place was jammed but few had taken their seats. Instead, a long line snaked all the way back to the vestibule in the front, leading up the left side aisle to the altar.

To the casket.

I got in back of a middle-aged woman in black hose with heels to match and scanned the crowd. So, who were all these people, the people in Himillsy's life? Well, unlike the world of Spear, Rakoff & Ware, this really *was* the cast of *The Man in the Gray Flannel Suit.* Except today the gray had faded to black. But otherwise here they were: the manor-born friends and neighbors Gregory Peck was coming home to, all those hours on the train. I didn't belong here—the only person I knew was, for Chrissakes, the deceased.

So I dredged up what I did know—things about Himillsy that they couldn't have: Did they know about Baby Laveen, the realistic baby doll she secretly carried around with her to help her cope with the death of her infant brother De Vigny? Did they know she wanted to open a combination barbershop and restaurant called Snippets, just so she could watch the customers try to pick the stray bits of hair out of their teeth? That she wanted to create a TV show called *People Are Awful,* in which ordinary contestants would earn cash and prizes by doing things like kicking the crutches out from underneath toddlers with polio? Or that she had plans to make a movie short of a man being mercilessly pelted with two stiletto-heeled pumps and call it *These Shoes Are Killing Me?* The strange fruits of her imagination, confided during the dark hours of our school days—they gave me entree, entitlement that this entire throng, with its perfect teeth and padlocked jaws, did not have.

And then, as the line inched further, I realized . . .

No. It couldn't be. My imagination playing cruel tricks in the suffocating heat. The casket was . . . open.

No. Unthinkable.

And I could just make out—there she lay, hands crossed over her chest. Oh. Oh. I snapped my head away, clamped my eyes shut.

How could they? Ghouls. Ghouls do this.

I can't. I will bolt from the line, right now. Excuse myself, back out of the church, onto the street, and run, run and not stop until none of this existed.

Himillsy: *Not so fast, Happy. Old chum. You're not going anywhere. You will wait patiently in line. You remember lines don't you, from school? Registration, frat parties, lunch, graduation. This is just another one. And you will wait in it, like you always have.*

For me. You have a promise to keep.

She was right. As ever. I was powerless to do anything other than her bidding. The queue inched forward. Dread. Sick dread. I kept my attention to the rear of the church, to the doors, to the plaque on the wall honoring the congregation's World War II dead.

What on earth compels allegedly civilized people to do this, to desecrate not just bodies, but our memories? I can't remember her this way, I can't. Please someone, something, make this go away.

A dead body. The first I'd ever see. And it has to be you, Mills. This was not how it was supposed to go.

Endless, terrible minutes, drawing forward until I couldn't avoid it anymore. The time had come. I was too close, there were people watching, I had to do the right thing, what was expected, I had to turn and look, look at—

And a burst of something like relief popped in my heart because, it . . . wasn't her.

Surprise! Nobody home! GOTCHA!!

It was what she'd left behind. So obvious. Mind you—the utter inhumanity of it, the ghastliness of the display was still appalling, but at least it wasn't *her.* Yes, her pixie features, the elegant fingers tapered pencil-thin, her aura of elfin beauty—they lingered like the glow of a candlewick after you blow the flame out. But Himillsy—*my* Himillsy—was long gone. This . . . remnant, it was not the person I knew. She would have agreed.

And can you believe this dress? I wouldn't be caught **dead** *in this thing!*

Didn't they know her? Didn't her own family even know anything about her? Mills, you of all people deserved better than this. Is that why you did it? Is that why you checked out, because this was the alternative?

The cliché is that dead people look like they're sleeping. They don't. That's a lie. Sleeping people vibrate despite themselves, with the ever-present promise of reanimation. Their vulnerability is tender, and fills you with the need to keep them safe. The dead just look exactly that. And they don't make you want to protect them. They make you want to take them out like the trash. Bury them. Or burn them—anything to return them to the earth, to get them out of your sight—because until you do it's that much less possible to remember they were ever alive.

Then, next to me to my right—a familiar voice, fermented by time, eerily sliced the air: "Isn't she beautiful? She's so beautiful . . . "

I turned, froze. Couldn't accept what I was seeing: Himillsy, at age fifty, bending over her twenty-five-year-old corpse. "So *beautiful* . . . "

Her mother. She had to be, the resemblance was supernatural. Except that she was Himillsy as Doris Day. In black taffeta. There was a hostess-in-fourth-gear quality to her, even in these horrific circumstances—a desperation for proper social procedure and ceremony—so unlike her daughter. "Come, come see her," she beckoned, her face folded in perfect grief as she reeled in the arm of a reluctant skinny blonde girl in a licorice linen shift. It was then that I looked back at the body. Mills was right: they'd slid her husk into a white, frilly, lacey number she would have described as a giant Victorian sneeze. The idea that that's what she'd be wearing for the rest of what amounts to eternity—she, who was style itself—was beyond contemplation.

Paying respect. This, all of this, was the opposite of anything like that. The real Himillsy would spring bolt upright, this very instant—not to bring any measure of assurance to the mourners, but to give them all a heart attack. Oh, if only.

I staggered away to the rear of the church and climbed the steps to the balcony, lost in repulsion and misery. I wanted to be as far away from it as possible. After another twenty minutes, with a mercy too long in the coming to ever redeem those responsible, the coffin lid was closed.

"All rise."

The rector read the prayer, then we recited the twenty-third Psalm, in unison. Like the docile, idiot lambs we were.

A hymn, "A Mighty Fortress Is Our God," and then it was time for what the program listed as "Reflections." There was only one name: LEVIN DODD. A young man got up and made his way hesitantly to the lectern.

Hmm. A cousin?

He was tall, slight. Early twenties, I'd say. My age. Delicate but sturdy, you could tell. He started, uneasily. "My sister, once made me promise,"

Sister. Levin, her brother, Levin. As in . . . Laveen? Impossible. Himillsy had told me he'd died. As an infant.

"–promise, she made me promise that–"

She'd said that his name was De Vigny, that she was too young to pronounce it correctly, that her father had given her a plastic replica of him as a solace. Baby Laveen. All a lie?

"–that if I was to ever, ever speak at her . . ." he popped an intake of breath, the sound of a bicycle tire giving out, "at her, fu . . ." He couldn't, not that word. "That I'd. That she. She wanted me to say . . . this."

He swallowed air, bracing himself. He was going to do this for her. No matter what. His eyes went skyward as he tried to clear his throat.

"Himillsy . . . loved *Life*,"

It was tortuous. For everyone.

"but,"

He was horrible to look at.

"she also,"

A mouse in a trap.

"she also had a subscription,"

Gnawing on its tail, clean through to escape. Bright pain.

". . . to *Time* magazine, too." He crumpled, in mortification, to the confusion of just about everybody. Except me.

And presto: The tears were released from my head. Yes, finally, that was Himillsy. Now *that* was her. For that split second, when he said it—that ridiculous, sophomoric nonsense—she was alive in the air. And just as quickly, like a small wisp of smoke, eaten by it

Good-bye, Hims.

Levin dabbed at his head with a handkerchief, collected himself with borrowed effort, and returned to his seat. The pipe organ kicked in, swelled—the strains of "How Great Thou Art." Everyone stood, opened to page 418, began to sing halfheartedly; the choir carrying it, covering for everyone.

THEN SINGS MY SOUL,

Hims, how could you do this to me? To all of these people? Look at them.

MY SAVIOR GOD, TO THEE,

You selfish, narcissistic, indulgent, self-obsessed, unforgivable bitch.

HOW GREAT THOU ART, HOW GREAT THOU ART!

It's my fault. I was too late. I should have gotten to you sooner, I could have saved you. I know it. I could have solved your problems. But I was a coward.

Himillsy. My little gumdrop in the mud. Smothered.

I closed the hymnal, managed to set it down on the pew. Then, untethered and all too connected, I shook. Uncontrollably. Helpless. As a piece of me—one of the best parts there ever would be—was ripped out, stolen, burned.

And buried.

• • •

They filed slow out of the church, the organ chords heavy as the air. The reception was in the adjoining parish room, but he cut through the crowd, slipped out the side door. I followed him. There, around to the rear of the building. Alone, leaning against the garbage bin, head hung, smoking. Unseen, I hesitated to approach. Was that really him?

It was wrong to trespass on this private moment. I had to. "P-pardon me." I tried to think of something unobtrusive to say. "Uh, do you have a light?"

His face was the color of marshmallow. "Sh. Sure." He offered his lighter just as I realized that I did not have a cigarette, seeing as I do not smoke. Pathetic. We stood like that for what seemed like minutes—his arm extended, brandishing the Zippo reluctantly, like he was showing a traffic cop his driver's license. Not looking at me, thoughts elsewhere. I felt like an utter, complete fool. Then he suddenly awoke to the situation.

"Oh. I *am* sorry, here." He handed me one of his Lucky Strikes, lit it.

I took it gratefully and introduced myself. He didn't seem to recognize my name. "We, Himillsy and I, were friends," I offered meekly, "at State, years ago. When she was a junior."

Levin's face flushed with dark recollection. He stared at the ground. "Millsy didn't talk much about school. Sore subject." There was something strangely familiar about him—he looked like someone I knew, but I just couldn't place it. Not like Himillsy, that wasn't it. Someone else.

"I, we, we just recently reconnected. We had lunch, were going to be in touch again. Look," I whispered, "Lord knows this isn't the time, but I'd really like to talk to you. Himillsy talked about you . . . all the time, and well." His head bolted up. "Well, I just really liked her a lot, I." And his eyes started to fill. "I mean, that sounds so dumb. 'Like' is such a dumb word," not just with tears but with something else. "I'm sorry. I wish I could explain it," with anger. "I wish I—"

"Did you see that dress?!" he spat. He was furious. At me? "Himillsy . . ." No, not at me. "She . . ." It was as if he suddenly knew that I was on his side. That we were against them, all of them. Whoever they were.

And then he was on me. Arms thrown around my neck, his head hard into my chest, practically beating my heart for me. Uncontrollable sobs.

I fought for words and lost. What is there, ever, to say in such a situation? That she would have wanted us to be strong?

Oh, please. "Strong" is for drinks. Be my guest—fall to pieces.

*It sure worked for **me**.*

• • •

"Plupp." Two days later. Sketch was erasing like a madman.

"Plupp, Plupp." A Krinkle ad, half-inked, trying to salvage it. And there goes the victorious beaming grin from the face of the potato chip god.

"Plupp, Plupp, Plupp." Gone is a good half of the adoring crowd.

"Plupp, Plupp, Plupp, Plupp." He tersely muttered it with each stroke, the agitation hot in his mouth.

But not an it. A he. For Leonard J. Plupp had entered our lives the day before, unbidden and hastily introduced, at our weekly client meeting with Dick. He was a good bit younger than Stankey, maybe thirty, if that. I figured him for some kind of apprentice tagalong, with Uncle Stankey showing him the ropes of the ad biz. I sort of felt sorry for him on sight, as an Oliver Twist's worth of Stankey-borne secretarial indignities filled my mind, most of them involving the management of his prodigious output of chip spit. Lenny didn't look too thrilled about the prospect, either—his face was a clenched fist, his eyes two thin strips of licorice whip. His slate gray worsted wool suit, despite its impeccable tailoring, still couldn't hide the fact that it didn't, well, suit him. It looked like a costume and not like clothes. And he smelled like a Vicks inhaler.

We were unveiling a month's worth of "snack-to-school!" ads for the fall. Sketch had practically killed himself on a series of autumn-themed adventures in comic strip form starring Krinkle Karl, the anthropomorphic potato chip he created in the 1940s and trotted out seasonally when the mood struck. The boards were absolutely stunning, with Karl krinkling his way into all kinds of exquisitely rendered mischief: passing notes to his sweetheart, Tessie Tuber, in class and getting caught; colliding with his best friend, Chauncey Cheesestick, during a football game and creating a new taste sensation (The Cheddertater! Touchdown!); raking all the leaves in Tatertown, only to have them jumped into by his nemesis, Pucky Pretzel, and scattered everywhere. Sketch really went all out on these, as he did every year. The detailing on the leaves alone made your eyes water. Tip's copy was charm itself.

Stankey was delighted. "Wowser, Sketch. Hot-CHA!" And then. Then he rotated his lumpy form to the young man to his right and dispatched what we hadn't yet understood to be the five single most gut-wrenching words in the English language:

"What do you think, Lenny?"

A smoldering pause. "Gee, what do I think?" The air in the room vanished. Sketch's face said it all: Why, exactly, do we give a thimble's worth of bat shit what this Lenny whoever-the-hell-he-is thinks?

Plupp cleared his throat. "What do *I* think?" He was calm, measured, his deep voice a jarring contrast to his reedy body. "I think Krinkle Kutt sales are stale."

Stankey's face fell. Was that supposed to be funny? Doubtful. One quickly surmised that for Leonard J. Plupp the concept of "funny" was reserved for unwelcome smells.

"Sprinkles!!" Tip stood in the doorway, arms outstretched, eyes hungry. "Oops. Is this a bad time?"

"Tip, this is Lenny Plupp." I watched his face betray a flutter of toxic amusement at the name. His glance bounced against mine for a split second, and: yes, we were going have *fun* with that one later. Oh, yes.

Dick stared at the floor, his massive breasts losing their daily, pendulous, war with gravity. "He's the new head of regional sales."

What? This twit? Impossible.

"I see," said Tip, beaming, oblivious to the events of the last five minutes. He looked over at the boards, and whistled. "God, I hadn't seen these finished yet." Which was a lie. Mr. Showman. He turned back to Plupp. "Aren't they sensational?"

"Well," said Lenny, "yes and no."

And Tip was speechless, for the first time that I'd ever seen.

"As examples of cartooning," Plupp continued,

soberly, "sensational they are. Utterly gorgeous. They always have been." Stankey stifled a spit. "But here are the facts: Sales of Krinkle products in this territory have been steadily declining for three years now. Which indicates that this cartoon approach is just not working anymore."

Sketch simmered, pipe clenched tightly in teeth. Reining it in. For now.

Because here was the thing about Sketch: He could and would denigrate his own work savagely, mercilessly, nearly out of existence. But if someone else did, look out. We had a lot of other accounts that were just busy work and we all knew that, but Krinkle was special. Krinkle was his valve—feeding his heart and releasing its boiler room's buildup of considerable steam. The Krinkle ads were sacred, untouchable.

Weren't they?

"Look," Lenny said, wearily pragmatic, "we'll go with a couple of these for now. We've got to run *something* starting tomorrow," shooting Dick an annoyed glance, "we've already paid for the space." He perched his hat on his head, signaled for Stankey to hustle up. "But I want this re-thought. And soon. Let's meet again in a week."

Maybe I was imagining it, but a thin, invisible fog of fear seemed to descend over the office. A hastily assembled, closed-door meeting in Mimi's office—to which I was not summoned—bore this out. No doubt about it: Lenny Plupp was trouble.

An hour afterward, with the phonograph cranked and Jelly Roll Morton restoring the calm, Sketch ruled up a board and scoffed. "Just another giggle-shit account rep in his tighty whites, doing cartwheels for Daddy. Seen a million of 'em."

Tip wasn't so sure. We discussed it the next day after Sketch left for lunch. "I'd agree, except Stankey is *deferring* to him. It would appear Pluppy's in charge. And if so, not good. The Meems will call in a cease and desist, but I don't like it, not one bit."

"Well, I—" My phone rang. Miss Preech: "There's a call for you on line one."

"Who is it, please?"

"A Mr. Dodd. He said it's important."

Whoa. I signaled to Tip that I needed to take it. He bolted. "Put him through, thanks . . . Hello?"

"Hi there."

"Levin."

"I'm sorry to bother you at work. I lost your home number. Is this an inconvenient time?" I'd given him my card before we parted. He sounded completely different now than at the funeral. Composed, sturdy, confident.

"No, not at all."

"I just wanted to apologize."

"Heavens, what for?"

"I made a damn fool of myself at the funeral."

"Oh, nonsense. Please, I mean—"

"Look, I've been thinking. It's not just that. I'm not going to be here much longer. I've got to get back to

Cambridge for the fall. There's something I want to talk to you about. But."

"What?"

He hesitated. "Not over the phone. You'd said about getting together. Let's meet for a drink?"

"Of course. Can you make it into New Haven?"

"That's fine. How's your Thursday?"

"Thursday's good. I get off work at six."

"Aces. Let's meet at the Taft. See you then."

The Tap Room at the Taft Hotel, on Chapel Street, was like every hotel bar at a university in the off-season. It reflected the gloom of lonely, well-heeled souls who take single rooms for the night. Deserted and bracing itself for the impending fall semester deluge. At six fifteen on Thursday, Levin was waiting for me in a booth in the rear. As he stood and we shook hands, exchanged muted greetings, I couldn't shake the feeling I was meeting a ghost. And that weird familiarity about him, I just couldn't place it. Maddening. After we ordered drinks I gathered the strength to speak before he had a chance to. "I need to ask you a very strange question, forgive me."

"Yes?"

"Did you and Himillsy have a little brother, named . . . De Vigny?"

All he was able to say, with squinted eyes, was, "You mean like the French poet?"

Well, that answered that. Would I have the guts to follow through with this, to tell him the truth? As in:

"Bingo! You see, Levin, in case you didn't know, at school your sister, that lovable kook, invented your death as an infant in order to fetishize you as a piece of uncannily molded rubber in the shape of a human baby, with which she then became psychotically obsessed. Yes, she was quite a card." Oh God. I would never have that kind of strength. Instead: "Yes, the French poet. Never mind. Uh, how about . . ."

"Hmm?"

"A rhinoceros head. Did she mention a rhinoceros head?"

That really, really alarmed him. And not because he knew what I was talking about. "A *what*?"

My line of questioning was not helping me. "Sorry, skip it. So, you were saying, on the phone?"

"Right. Well, I know this is going to sound bonkers. But."

A pause. I didn't dare interrupt.

"I really thought about this. It's been all I've been able to think about for days, Christ knows. And I want you to keep this quiet. Not that you'd." He was keeping the tears at bay. Just barely. "I mean, I have reason to believe . . . " Then he brought himself to look me in the eyes.

". . . Himillsy wasn't trying to kill herself. Not really."

Uh-huh. She just locked herself in the garage and gunned the engine of her Corvair and went to sleep forever in order to live life to the fullest. Levin, you poor thing.

I did not say this. I didn't have to.

"Look, I just thought you should know that." Reversion: He was the distraught little boy at the funeral again.

"But what. I mean, why do—"

"Because Mums—I mean, my mother—was due home that day at six. From tennis. She always is, on Fridays, like clockwork."

"I don't understand."

"I'm sorry. I'm not being clear. I really don't know who else to talk to about this. I've just been so frazzled, and here I nearly tackled you after the service."

"Please, not another word about that. It was perfectly natural." Sort of. But regardless, it bound us together, and I needed it. I'd grown deeply grateful for it, actually. In the past week since the funeral I'd convinced myself that Levin and I were the only two people there, the only two in the world, who really mourned her properly. The only ones who understood.

"Thanks." He absentmindedly took the salt cellar from its little wire cage. "I don't know how much you know, but I take it Millsy's death really hit you hard, too, so I wanted to tell you this." And shook a thin layer of white crystals onto the table next to his glass. "The cops estimate she started the engine sometime between five thirty and six. Mums should have walked right into it. It's so obvious." He slowly ran his finger through it, forging a path. "But she didn't."

"Why not?"

"Christ. Bunny Williams asked her over for post-match stingers to see her new dahlia beds. With Pops away at a conference, and me gone to the Cape for the weekend, she didn't see the harm."

"Oh, Jesus."

"She didn't make it home till eight." Scarcely a whisper: "That was that."

Silence.

Which I then broke. "So you think that . . ."

"I think she wanted," he closed his eyes, made himself say it: "Himillsy wanted to be saved. By *her.*" There was more than a little anger coursing through that last sentence. As in "not *me.*"

I knew exactly how he felt.

So much for staving off the tears, which he dabbed with a napkin. "I truly believe that. That's what's so unbearable. They were always at each other's throats, and I think this was her way of saying, 'I want to start over.' I know that sounds crazy."

"No. Not . . . " Not for her. How to say it with any tact? "Not . . . completely. I wonder . . ."

"What."

"Well, had they fought recently? Was this a response to something like that?"

"No, you see, that's the thing. They hadn't had one of their dustups in an age. And yet," he stumbled over the words, "at the same time . . . something *was* eating at her. I could see it. In the last couple of weeks. Something more than usual."

And that was saying a lot. Upon reflection, during the remaining years of school it became obvious that

Himillsy was fueled as much by demons as she was by her considerable creative fire. What exactly they were and where they came from I couldn't say, but there was definitely some kind of perpetual war she was waging. With her teachers, with her boyfriend Garnett, ultimately with me. No one was spared, not even herself. And now I saw: That went double for her family; Levin, too. That was the origin of his ineffable sadness. To look at him was to visit the sorry source of doomed devotion itself. To recognize what a glorious pinprick it was to love Himillsy.

Like looking into a mirror. "Do you have any idea what it was?"

"No, I've been racking my brain." He lit a Lucky Strike, offered me one. Which I took, for consistency's sake. "If anything, things were looking up. She was doing a little painting again. She was enrolled in some correspondence art courses, which we'd been at her to do for years. She was finally back on track to get a degree."

I am dirt. I am the worst person in the world. I have failed you, Hims. Again. I would have been there at six on the dot. I swear. I would have eagerly trampled Bunny Williams's dahlia-choked corpse to get to you.

Ahem. So why didn't you, exactly?

Now wait a minute. That is not fair.

"Um, would you like another?" Levin's voice rang like a referee's bell, signaling the end of this round. He waved to the bartender.

"Oh. Sure. Sorry about that. Drifted there a sec."

We needed to talk about something else. I asked him what was in Cambridge. He was about to start his second year at Harvard Law, with a concentration on copyright legislation. He was as sharp and focused as Himillsy was adrift. At close to eight thirty he looked at his watch.

"Shoot. Gotta run."

Rats. There was so much more I wanted to tell him. I gathered that Himillsy led a rather segregated life, and he didn't seem to know much about anything that happened to us at State. I thought he'd get a kick out of hearing about it. Perhaps another time, which probably meant never. He paid the tab, ignoring my protests to at least split it, and I walked him to the parking lot.

We stopped at a storm-sky blue MGA roadster. Leather interior the shade of bricks in the late-afternoon sun. Another world. I shook his hand. "Listen, thanks. Thanks for telling me that. It."

He waited for me to continue. I think he knew where this was going.

"It helps me," now I was going to cry. Don't, don't. "Helps me to forgive her." I wiped my eyes as inconspicuously as possible.

"Yes, that's it exactly," he said, sniffling. "That's what I was hoping." He fumbled with his keys, opened the door. "Keep in touch." The way he said it, I rather doubted I'd ever see him again. Everything about him said he was eager for a life away from here, now with more reason than ever.

And as he folded himself into the driver's seat of the compact, I finally figured out who he looked like, why he made me so sad, who he reminded me of. A mirror, yes.

It was me.

• • •

At the office a week later, I was just about to dash out for a quick bite at Louie's Lunch when Tip stuck his head in the door and announced, in his best Jeeves voice:

"La Goddessa would like a word with you."

Miss Preech. If it was ever true that a woman could be beautiful only when she was angry, then Miss Preech was absolutely ravishing, twenty-four hours a day. Tip had christened her "the Goddess of Love," which eventually evolved into "la Goddessa d'Amor," then just shortened to Goddessa. Hers was a realm ruled with exquisite displeasure.

Damn. What did I do now? When I got to her desk she was polishing off a tuna sandwich with the crusts trimmed and scanning *TV Guide*. She leveled her gaze at me with mild irritation and plucked something up from a pile of grocery circulars.

"Do you want me to mail this? You forgot to put postage on it." A standard letter-size envelope, with a "return to sender" mark where the stamp should be.

My head, jammed with a catalog's worth of layout schemes for next week's circular for the Food Clown's

Bulk Bargain Blowout, alloyed with the ever-present desire to escape the piercing plain of the Goddessa's thoughts altogether, led me to issue a terse, "Sure. Thanks."

But by the time I was halfway to George Street, my brain was filing the catalog away for safe keeping, and underneath it lay the envelope.

Which I had no memory of.

One of the simple perks of working at an office is personal use of its services, of which I almost never took advantage. As opposed to Tip, who would have had every tooth in his head ripped out and replaced with filed and polished shards of platinum if he thought he could charge it to the Sparklebrite toothpaste account. But I hadn't yet grown the guts to send private correspondence through the agency. So what was that letter? I hadn't studied it carefully at all, but the addressee and the return address had been handwritten. Which . . . I had seen before. I knew that now.

I was already turned back, pace quickening exponentially, as I tried to make sense of things. Something about it was registering panic. I had to see that letter again. I *had* to.

I sprinted the last block. Breathless, buzzing my way in. "Miss Preech, have you sent that letter?"

Dictaphone clinging to her head for dear life, fingers dancing on hot coal keys, she announced, not deigning to look at me, "It hasn't been picked up yet."

"Thank GOD," I said, too loudly. "I mean, could I take a look at it? I need to check something."

She tilted her frosted pate at the out mailbox. With a sense of guilt whose origins I couldn't name, I plucked it, for inspection. And my blood became ether.

The handwriting was Himillsy's.

The return address read my name, care of the firm. The addressee was:

H. DODD INDUSTRIES, INC.
Guilford, Conn. 06378

I staggered up the steps to my desk. How, how could this be? I laid it on my drawing table gently, like it was a Fabergé egg. Or a time bomb. Was I supposed to send this back to her? No wait, that didn't make sense. No, this was her way of sending something to *me*. But what?

The impulse to just let it lie there and remain forever unopened held the allure of vicarious superiority.

Right. Like you're going to do that.

Damn. I took my X-Acto knife and tremulously slit it up the right side, opposite the return address. I bowed the envelope and shook out the contents. Two pieces of paper floated onto the desk. One was folded.

It was the ad. *My* ad, for the Yale psych experiment, clipped from the *Register*. The other was a recipe torn from *McCall's* magazine, with the headline "Lemon Sandies to Die For!" Under which it had been scrawled, with a red pen, in Himillsy's unmistakably manic hand:

That was it. No note, nothing else.

So much for forgiveness. The questions took over.

How did she send it to me without paying postage? And from beyond the grave?

Self-explanatory. Our fine postal pushers aren't exactly smart enough to send Sputnik into orbit. I sent this weeks ago. Then they bounced it back to where they thought it came from originally. I knew it would take those chowderheads forever to process it. And I wasn't supposed to croak in the first place, remember?

What did it mean, what was I supposed to do with it?

Well now, that's for you to figure out, isn't it?

Was this just a dumb joke, or was she trying to tell me something? And if so, WHAT, for Chrissakes?

See above, dick stain. Besides, you're only imagining all of these answers anyway. Adios for now! Vaya con queso!

Bitch. Unforgivable bitch.

My first thought was to call Levin. And I almost did. But with my finger hovering over the dial I thought better of the idea. It wasn't like I'd received a coherent, impassioned good-bye letter, which wouldn't have been her style anyway. It was a confusing, baffling, reminder of her questionable sanity. And Levin's life was troubled enough. Why inflict this on him? No.

I decided: This gesture, whatever it meant (probably nothing), was between Himillsy and me, period.

It would be best that way. Best forgotten as soon as possible.

• • •

"Here's to you, maestro of the marking pen." Tip clinked his martini glass into Sketchy's frosted mug of Rheingold ale.

"Hear hear! Many happy returns," I followed suit with my gin and tonic.

"Skol," he said, quietly.

Sketch famously hated any sort of fuss whatsoever on his birthday, but Tip managed to talk him into allowing the two of us to take him after work to his favorite dive bar, Saluzo's, on Wooster Street in Little Italy. Great burgers, white paper tablecloths just perfect for doodling, and best of all for Tip—the perfect name. "It sounds like some juiced-up lush trying to pronounce 'sleazy losers.' Genius."

"Lookin' good, Speary." Billy Saluzo Jr., the barkeep, gave us the thumbs-up. "First round on the house."

"Yes, I honestly don't know how you do it, Sketcher," purred Tip, "you look like a million lire."

"Don't listen to him." I gave Sketch's arm a gentle nudge. "How does it feel to be fifty-seven?"

"Heh. Just a smidge better than it will feel to be fifty-eight. If I live that long."

"God, and I'm going to be forty any minute. It's tragic." Tip frowned. "Do you realize that when Mozart was my age he'd already been dead for five *years?*"

I couldn't resist. "And you're going to join him soon if you keep chain-smoking like that."

"Oh, tosh. Do you want to know something?" Some people spoke volumes. Tip spoke leaflets. "You don't actually live longer by giving up smoking. It just *seems* longer." He ignited the end of a Pall Mall in defiance. "Honestly, if I read one more thing about the possible effects of smoking, I'm going to give up reading."

"Here, Sketch," I said, removing a manila envelope from my knapsack. "It's not much. I only found out yesterday it was your birthday. Sorry." I slid it across the table.

"Hey. Hey, you didn't need to do that."

"Wait'll you see it." I laughed, all nerves. "Then you'll *really* think so." Please like it. Oh, *please.*

He opened the flap and gently slid out the drawing I'd been up till three trying to make into something worthy of him. And failing miserably, of course. "Heh. Would ya look at that. Your shading's getting better."

Originally I was going to try do Little Nemo meeting Krinkle Karl in Slumberland, but there wasn't time. So instead I'd drawn a hyper-detailed Baby Laveen, brushes in one hand and palette in the other, bowing regally before the feet of an otherwise unseen master, towering above him. The caption read

A SKETCH IS WORTH A THOUSAND WORDS.
HERE'S THE FIRST TWO: BIRTHDAY. HAPPY.

Sketch whistled. "That's darn good."

"No it's not, really. But at least it's proof that I'm practicing, right? Every night, really."

"Say, that *is* pretty good, Hap," said Tip, trying to pull Billy's attention from the Yankees game on the TV under the cash register, "maybe we could use it on—"

"Hot-cha!" Dick Stankey burst through the door. Sketch's face lit up. He slipped the drawing back into the envelope and bolted up from the table.

"Stankey! You bastard!" I'd never seen him so glad to see anyone. Tip must have called and invited him. They hugged, as if they hadn't seen each other in months. "What'll it be, piss or vinegar?"

"Hah! What the heck—a Manhattan. With a lot of cherries!"

"Billy," Tip called, "make it so. And another for me."

With Dick's drink plopped in front of him, talk turned to his family, the weather, and the Yankees' playoff prospects—everything but what was begging, finally, to be discussed. We all strenuously avoided it.

Except Tip. Well into his second martini, he decided to acknowledge the elephant in the room. "So, Stanker, what's the skinny on the new skinny?"

Silence.

Tip, Jesus. Not here, not now.

Stankey rebounded with strained ebullience. "What, Lenny? Oh, he's just a big noise." A snort. "And talk about dumb—he has to pull out his dork just to count to eleven. Eh, Sketch?" Yucks all around, but there was no hiding it: the faint yet unmistakable odor of desperation wafting off his pasted-on smile. He would not concede to it, not tonight. Change of subject. "Hey Sketch, remember Krinkle in the old days, with Lars?"

And it popped, unbidden, into my mind:

m e m o r y.

Stop. Stop it. I will not think of it.

"Heh, oh yeah." Sketch chuckled. "He was a quick study, that's for sure."

s t u d y   o f   m e m o r y.

This was happening more and more in the last two days, ever since I received Himillsy's letter—pieces of the Yale psych ad, inserting themselves into my thoughts, into conversation, triggered by any related phrases. It was as if Tip's word-association game had taken over my mind.

"I sure learned a lot from him."

m e m o r y   a n d   l e a r n i n g.

Enough. I will put an end to this, now.

"Sketch," I said, "tell me something about Lars. What was he like to work with?"

"Heh. Lars." He lit up his pipe, thought a moment. "The thing about Lars was, he could look inside you, and it was like he was trying to find something. And then he would. And then he wanted to mine it and refine it and use it. And the thing was, you really *wanted* him to. Because God knows you couldn't."

"Yeah, he was the goods," said Dick, crunching his maraschino cherries. "Remember that time he ran that joke ad on April Fool's Day about the all-you-can-eat chips contest? We sold tons! And no prize money! That was a pisser!" He snorted, shook his head. Then, "Holy buckets! Look at the time. Hey gang, gotta run. Happy returns, Sketch. What am I owe ya?"

"Eh, your dough's no good here," he grinned, "you big sissy."

They hugged again, and Stankey was off.

Sketch excused himself to the men's. I turned to Tip. Something I'd been wanting to know for a while now: "Does Sketch have any family? What's that story?"

His face darkened. "Oh, I guess he didn't tell you yet. It's so sad," he sighed. "He's been a widower for almost twenty years now. His dear sweet Mairley died in childbirth. He lost them both."

"Oh my God. He never said a word of it."

"He doesn't advertise it." Tip didn't seem to recognize the pun. "He waited a good two years before he told me." A cheer from the TV. Score one for the

Yanks. "But I'll never forget it, when he told me, the way he said it." He took his eyes away from mine. I saw the threat of actual tears. "He said . . . 'I became one sock.' "

. . .

The next morning Mimi called another Krinkle strategy meeting. And I formed a little strategy of my own. After I heard her office door close, I took my coffee mug and went downstairs, past Miss Preech, and into the pantry. I poured a cup, then stealthily opened the rear exit on the other side and mounted the service stairway to the second floor. Once the coast was clear, I tiptoed down the hallway to Mimi's office and planted my back to the wall to see what I could hear. As luck would have it, the milk-glass transom above the doorjamb was cracked open a good six inches and I could just make out their conversation.

"—we need to convince this Lenny that we're on his side," said Nicky, "that we want to sell to the widest possible audience."

And bang, it flashed, again:

Factory Workers
City Employees
Laborers
Barbers
Businessmen
Clerks
Professional People
Telephone Workers
Construction Workers

Salespeople
White-collar Workers
Others

Stop thinking about it. Stop it. Forget it.

Mimi: "*I* know . . ." a pause, "I want you to start thinking about Krinkle Karl as someone adults could look up to. Maybe even ask for advice. Yes! That's it — like Monsignor Sheen. Or J. Edgar Hoover. Of course!"

"Great idea, Mummy." Every time Nicky referred to Mimi this way, I never failed to think: Goodness, that's not very nice. Yes, the resemblance to Boris Karloff is undeniable, but she IS your mother.

"Thank you, Nicky. Poopy, what do you think?"

Poopy? Who the hell was Poopy?

Preston: "For two cents I'd tell 'em all to go pound sand!"

Mimi sniffed. "Poop, that's not going to help the cause."

"If I may," said Tip, "this all points to what I've been saying all along: Ads don't sell products, *stores* sell products. Right?"

Nicky, irritated: "Oh, not this again."

"I'm sorry, but it's true. All an ad can do is give you a *need* for something . . .

Persons needed

". . . to plant the seed of inquiry, the quest for knowledge . . ."

for a study

". . . about something you didn't realize you needed in the first place. Or something you forgot."

of memory

I couldn't escape it: anything I heard, read, or saw held a connection to it. Himillsy, why did you send it to me, why?

There are no further obligations.

Forget it. Let it go.

Except.

Oh come ON, you ding-a-ling.

Unless I'm not supposed to let it go at all. Is that it, Hims, just the opposite, because you . . . did you?

I've been doing brain exercises, remember?

Nicky: "Look, I have a lunch. We'll continue this later. Sketch, get working on some new ideas, please, thanks." Meeting adjourned. I bolted up the steps and back to my desk.

And dialed for an outside line. I still had the number, thumbtacked to the edge of my pencil tray. Please still be in town, *please* . . .

"Hello?"

Thank God. "Levin."

"Oh, hi. Didn't think I'd hear from you so soon."

"Yeah, sorry about that. Listen, I just have a quick question, I hope that's all right."

"Sure."

"I'm sorry if it's painful. It's sort of important, to me."

" . . . Okay."

"Did Himillsy say anything about, well, something she did at Yale, maybe a few weeks ago? About . . . a study she might have participated in? With the psych department. Does that ring a bell?"

"Hmm. Let me think."

I waited.

"I, come to think of it," he said, slowly, "she joked one afternoon that she was going in to the Yale psych department for some tests. I assumed it was a gag, or an art thing, but . . . " Then, he continued, with just a hint of suspicion, "How did you know that?"

Oops. Think. "She'd . . talked to me about maybe doing something like that. That day we had lunch."

"Huh. Well, I would say it's a strong possibility." There was something new in his voice. Irritation. "Look, I've got to run." As in *Don't call me again.*

"Yes, of course. Thanks so much."

Click.

As I started to sketch out the headline for a "white" sale for Sparklebrite toothpaste, I looked over at the stack of *Register* pages, neatly folded. And I asked myself: When I designed that ad, what was I doing, on behalf of the client?

I was trying to start a conversation.

And maybe the problem was . . . I hadn't finished it. I'd abandoned it. Tip was right: Most of the ads we did posed strictly rhetorical questions. We never *really* knew the extent to which any of them reached anybody. Lenny Plupp didn't understand that. But my psych ad required an actual, physical response. Maybe that's what Himillsy was trying to say: Wasn't I somehow morally obligated to see it through? How could I demand this of the general public and not myself? Doesn't this go to the very heart of what advertising is? What it can do?

The answer: Answer it.

Well, finally. It took you long enough to figure that one out, Einstein.

There was no way I was going to be free from this until I went through with it. Until I . . .

. . . filled it out.

I want to take

. . . clipped it.

part in this study

. . . mailed it.

of memory and learning.

For the next three days, every time the phone rang, it held the promise of

PUBLIC
ANNOUNCEMENT

and then broke it: "Mr. Spear, please."

Until it kept it: "Hello? I'm calling from Yale University."

Finally. The next day, at the appointed hour, I looked at the address to the laboratory I'd written on the back of a Pepe's Pizza receipt, and then at the building marked Linsley-Chittenden Hall. A neo-Gothic pile of coffin-size blocks. Laboratory? No.

A cathedral.

Okay, so here I am, Himillsy. To test my memory. Is that what you wanted? Is this really necessary?

Because, you must know by now· You *already* test my memory.

Every single day.

• • •

CONTENT, THE KEY INGREDIENT.

We'll get back to our regularly scheduled program in just a moment, but first I'd like to take a few seconds of your time to introduce myself. Perhaps you know me from one of my many appearances in print, radio, movies, television, heck—even human beings! My name is Content. You're probably familiar with my more recognizable partner, Form, while I remain something of a mystery. So I thought I'd take out a few of these paid "spots" to help clarify what I am and what I can do—for your clients, your business, even for yourself! There are so many answers.

But before we get to those, let me recap a bit and remind you that all media—especially, for our purposes, Graphic Design—can be divided into Form and Content. However, the real revelation is that so can I, Content itself, be divided—into what I Say and what I Mean. For example, on this page, what you're seeing is a series of abstract symbols (letters) connected in specific ways (Form), but what you're perceiving is the message that I'm using them to tell you (Content). But get this: That message can then be further processed in any number of ways to fully understand it. And your brain performs all sorts of tricks to achieve this.

You probably hear me as a voice in your head this second. Isn't that amazing? But here's the big question: What am I really telling you? And no, what I Say and what I Mean are not always the same thing—heck, rarely—as we'll see later.

Well. We're just getting started, and that's about all the time I have for now. I'll be checking in again soon, though, in another of my various incarnations.

Now, back to our show . . .

II.

DURING.

1 9 6 1

S E P T E M B E R .

"Have a seat here, please."

So this was Yale. The imposing facade of Linsley-Chittenden Hall gave way to the lab's more modest entrance around the side—a small cobwebbed set of concrete stairs that led to the basement, through a dusty corridor bleached with makeshift overhead lighting, finally into a receiving area, a door marked INTERACTION LABORATORY. This room, this engine of Old Blue, was festooned with taupe lisle curtains, gray linoleum floors dotted with specks of ruby, a large dusky mirror in a wood frame on the far wall. Not the great hall I was expecting. But I felt it anyway: Ivy everywhere. This was the real thing. Science itself.

"I'm Mr. Williams." The man in the gray lab coat steered me to an office chair not unlike mine at work—forest green Naugahyde swirl, brushed aluminum frame, wheels.

"Here we are." He was thin as a pin, a lonely lock

of hair combed over his otherwise bald head. Ichabod Crane.

Another man, stocky and then some, thick horn-rimmed glasses, mid-forties, was led into the room, sat. Looked a bit like Sketch, actually—generous cheeks, clean-shaven, hair gray at the temples, business attire. He was introduced as Mr. Wallace. I leaned over to him, shook his fleshy hand.

Ichabod: "Okay, you've both answered the ad we've placed in the paper and will be participating in our study of memory. Now, as of this point both of you have been paid, so let me say that the checks are yours just for showing up at the lab. No matter what happens now, the money is yours."

Which I hadn't even considered at all. Who cared about the money? That's not why I was here.

"Before we get started, I'd like to tell you both a little about the memory project." He cleared his throat, crossed his hands before him. He was due for a nail clipping but otherwise groomed to a paranormal degree, clinically sterile. Though clearly striving for civility, he shot us a cold, hard stare—we were amoebas in a petri dish under his microscope. I already imagined we'd be asked to memorize entire pages of text and would be found wanting. Just being back in any kind of school classroom situation was enough to bring back that old institutional anxiety.

"Psychologists have developed several theories to explain how people learn various types of material.

One theory is that people learn things correctly whenever they get punished for making a mistake."

Punished.

"Like when a parent spanks a child when he does something wrong. But actually, we in the scientific community know very little about the effect of punishment on learning, because almost no documented studies have been made on human beings. For instance, we don't know how much punishment is best for learning, and we don't know how much difference it makes as to who's giving the punishment—whether an adult learns best from an older or younger person and many things of this sort. So what we're doing with this project is bringing together a number of adults, of different occupations and ages, and are asking some of them to be teachers, and some to be learners. We want to find out just what effect people will have on each other as teachers and learners, and also what effect punishment will have on learning in this situation."

What was all of this about punishment? There was nothing about it in the ad. I should know.

"Therefore I'm going to be asking one of you to be the teacher here this afternoon, and the other to be the learner." Before I could raise my hand he pulled two folded pieces of paper from his pocket, the size and shape of Chinese cookie fortunes. "And the way we usually decide who is who is to let you to draw from these. One of them says 'learner' and the other one says 'teacher.' "

I already knew which one I wanted. He crumpled

them up and cupped them in his hands, shook them, offered. We each took one.

"Can you open those, and tell me which of you is which, please?"

I did. Not what I wanted. Dammit. "Teacher," I said. "Learner," said Wally.

"Um," I offered meekly, "sorry, but could we switch? I mean, I wanted to do this to test my memory. That's why I answered the ad." Not entirely true, but still.

Williams didn't like the idea. At all. "No sir. Rules are rules. You're the teacher." As if it were insulting that I'd even suggest it. Fine.

"Now, the next thing we have to do is set the learner up so he can receive punishment. Learner, will you step out here with me, please?"

He led Wally through a doorway to a small anteroom adjacent to the main lab, then popped his head back through the door, at me. "Teacher, you may look on if you want, while we get set up in here." It was more order than suggestion. There was something about this guy's voice—his dismissive and technical manner—it was very persuasive almost despite itself. Like a human traffic light. Go.

Wally was seated, made himself comfortable in the small room, which reminded me of the DJ booth at the State U radio station. A long metal countertop ran the length of it, and another mirror, like the one in the lab, lined the far wall. "You can leave your coat on the back of the chair. That's it. Pull up to the counter.

Good. Now, will you roll up your right sleeve, please? Great. What I'm going to do is strap down your arms to avoid any excess movement on your part during the experiment."

Excessive movement?

"Is that too tight?"

Thick leather straps with buckles, like belts, held Wally's meaty, wooly forearms fast to the counter in front of him. Then Ichabod attached a wire to Wally's right wrist.

"This electrode is connected to the shock generator in the next room."

Shock generator? What shock generator?

"And this electrode paste will provide a good contact, to avoid any blisters or burns."

Blisters or burns. Please. Such *drama.* He smeared the gluelike goo on Wally's fat wrist, a thin bracelet of guck.

"Now let me explain to you, Learner, exactly what's going to happen, what you're supposed to do. The teacher will be in the next room. He will read a list of word pairs to you like these: BLUE ball, NICE day, FAT head, and so forth."

FAT head. Wally!

"You are to try and remember each pair. For the next time through, the teacher will read only the first word—the first half—of the word pair. For example, he will say BLUE. Then he will read four other words, such as: boy, ball, grass, hat. Your job is to remember which one of these four other words was originally paired with BLUE. You'll indicate your answer by pressing one of these four switches. Can you reach those all right?"

Wally put out his hand to what looked like a small ham radio with the casing removed. There were four numbered levers jutting out of the front of it. He tested them.

"That's fine. Now if the first word I just read, BOY, had been paired with BLUE, you'd press the first switch to indicate to the teacher that you thought it was the first word. If you thought it had been the second word, BALL, then you'd press the second switch and so forth—the third word the third switch and the fourth word the fourth switch. Now, if you get it correct, fine. But if you make an error, you will be punished with an electric shock."

Ha!

"So, naturally it is to your advantage to learn all the word pairs as quickly as possible."

Wary Wally: "I should think *so*."

"Now, do you have any questions before we go into the next room?"

"No, but I, I should tell you this:" he hesitated, embarrassed, "a few years ago, three, I think, I was in the VA Hospital in West Haven, and they detected a slight heart condition. Nothing serious, but," he was getting twitchy, "as long as I'm having these shocks . . . "

"Yes?"

"How strong are they? How . . ."

Oh, *Wally*. Don't be such a baby. This was obviously a formality, just Yale covering all the bases. Besides, that gut of yours looks like it could absorb a *thunderstorm*. Stop worrying. This was going to be fun.

". . . how dangerous are they?"

"They may be painful."

That's why they call them shocks, you dope. Williams was too professional to roll his eyes, but he might as well have. "But they're not dangerous."

Of course not. This was a *lab*. At *Yale*.

"Anything else?"

"No, that's all."

"All right, Teacher, would you take the test please and be seated in front of the shock generator in the next room?" He handed me a sheaf of papers, closed the door on Wally, led me back to the main room. "This machine generates electric shocks."

Whoa. It wasn't in view when I first came in. Look at *that*.

It was like a hi-fi set the size of an upright piano, but with a long row of Bakelite toggle buttons across it all marked with voltage numbers. The switches were labeled in groups of four: SLIGHT SHOCK, MODERATE SHOCK, STRONG SHOCK, VERY STRONG SHOCK, INTENSE SHOCK, EXTREME INTENSITY SHOCK, DANGER: SEVERE SHOCK. Two switches after that were marked XXX. There was a microphone to the left of the machine, and another box atop it with the numbers 1, 2, 3, 4.

In the upper-left corner of the brushed-aluminum front panel, it said SHOCK GENERATOR, TYPE ZLB. DYSON INSTRUMENT COMPANY,

WALTHAM, MASS., OUTPUT 15 VOLTS -- 450 VOLTS.

The entirety of the typography on the device was set in all-caps medium weight Helvetica, a recently introduced Swiss font commonly used for utilities and municipal signage. I wondered if Ichabod knew that. Bet he didn't.

"When you push one of the switches all the way down, the learner gets a shock." He pushed one, marked 300 VOLTS. "When you release it, the shock stops, you see." He eased up on it, and instead of going back up all the way, it rose to mid-level. "The switch will remain in this middle position after you've released it to show you which switches you've used on the board. Of course, if you were to press any one of them again, the learner would get another shock." He flipped up the master switch. A slight hum from the cabinet. Lights on. A voltage meter came to life and woke its needle. "Okay, the machine is now on. To give you, the teacher, an idea of how much shock the learner is getting, we think it's only fair to give you a sample shock yourself. Are you agreeable to this?"

We think it's only fair. *We.* Ichabod and who? Yale? Hmmm. "Sure."

"Would you roll up your right sleeve please?"

I held it out to him. He smeared some of that goop on my wrist, placed an electrode on it. "I'm going to ask you to close your eyes and estimate the number of volts you receive in this sample shock. Do not open your eyes until I tell you to do so, please. Close them now." I did. "Ready?"

"Oka—"

Bzzzt. Hey now. I don't know much about electricity, but that was weird. A tickle pinprick. And *strong.*

"Okay, you may open your eyes." He wiped the paste off with a wet towel. "Using the voltage scale on the generator, estimate for me how many volts you think you received."

I looked at the scale. I hadn't a clue, but it *had* to be from the mid-to-high range. "One, one—ninety-five, two-hundred?"

"No, actually it was forty-five. Here." He pointed to the third button in. The *third.* In a series of *thirty.*

"You're joking."

He ignored me. "All right, let's go on to the instructions."

I rubbed my wrist, to massage the memory of the pain away. It wasn't working.

We went over the procedure again. I was to read the list of word pairs into the microphone, receive Wally's response on the number box, and if he was wrong, say so. Then announce the voltage and . . . shock him. For just a tiny split second.

"It's important that you follow the procedure exactly."

"Right. Uh—" What if something goes wrong? What then?

"Yes?"

"Nothing. Sorry."

Ichabod leaned into the mic. "Attention, Learner: the teacher is about to begin the word test. Please try and remember the word pairs." To me: "Now, we begin with fifteen volts."

But that's only if he screws it up. He'll be fine.

"And move up one switch, each time he gets a wrong answer."

Which he won't.

"Ready, begin please."

I looked at the list: Would I remember these? I thought so. They were set, by the way, in what appeared to be 36-point Bodoni Oldface BE Regular. Although it could have been forty point. Not a great print job. Anyway, I tried to read everything as slowly and clearly as possible. Give the guy a fair shot. "Hello, Mr. Wallace—Learner. Listen, please, okay? BLUE ball. NICE house. FAT head. GREEN paint. RICH man. FAST car. BLUNT words. SOFT blanket. COOL air. GOLD thread. HARD stone. WET fish. BRAVE girl. WHITE house. SAD story. SHORT trip. SHARP cheese. SLOW car. RED brick. LOW light. NEW day. QUIET time. TAME dog. TRUE love. SWEET thing.

"Got that?" Wally! "Okay?" I said it the way my dad used to right before we'd set off for a long car trip: "Here we go. BLUE: sky, ball, shirt, bird."

Bing. He pressed 2. Good.

"Very good. Next one. NICE: salary, dream, house, man."

Bing. He pressed 3. Good.

"Great! FAT: pig, chance, Tuesday, head."

Bing. 2. Not so good.

"Uh, that's wrong." I looked up at the face of the machine, then over at Ichabod. I was really on stage here. "Fifteen volts." I put my finger on the lever. Cold plastic the color of a dark sea. It gave way easily.

Bzzzt.

A small red light bloomed, the volt-meter spasmed. And yes, I admit: I laughed. A little chuckle. I don't know why. It wasn't because I thought it was funny, really.

Well, maybe a little. Onward. "GREEN: grass, man, lawn, paint."

Bing. 2. Green man? What a dope. "Wrong. Green paint. Thirty volts." Take that, Wally.

Bzzzt.

He got the next two right. The punishment theory was on the money—this would be smooth sailing now. Over within five minutes. "Excellent. Very good. BLUNT: words, instrument, knife, object."

Bing 4 Hmmm. "Wrong. Blunt words. Forty-five volts." The level of shock I had gotten. Wake up, Wally.

Bzzzt.

"SOFT: blanket, pillow, soap, song." Come *on.*

Bing. 3. What? "No. Sorry. Soft blanket. Suh, sixty volts."

Bzzzt.

This went on for the next three answers. Wrong, wrong, wrong. Wally, what the heck is your problem? He was rolling around in there. Bored, that's all. He'd shape up soon. He *had* to. "One hundred and five volts."

Bzzzt.

"Ow."

Waitaminute. Muffled, but unmistakable.

Williams scribbled something on his clipboard. I was afraid to look him in the eye, but, when I did it was . . . okay. He wasn't mad at me at all. Not disappointed in the least. Whew.

"WET: fish, coat, lip, stone."

Bing. 3. What was he doing in there? Wally, what the hell? "Muh, Mr. Williams, sir? Something's wrong. He's getting them all wrong."

"Keep going. Go on, please."

Bzzzt.

"Oh!"

I started to think up things to help him, anything— I drew out the correct word, emphasized it to tip him off: "*Ssstooooonne . . .*"

"Please don't try to cheat, Teacher." Damn.

Bzzzt.

"*OW!*"

Christ. And then I thought of Himillsy for the first time since the experiment began. Which one of us had she been? Did she sit in the same chair I was in right now? What would she do in this situation? Maybe the sound system was spotty. I leaned heavy into the mic, nearly shouting: "Are you hearing me okay? Mr. Wallace?" Nothing. To Williams. "Maybe he can't hear me. We, we should check that."

"The equipment is fine. Please continue."

How could he be so sure? So sure of everything? But he *was,* and I realized, yes, I was grateful for that—

in the way I always was for people who were obviously smarter than I am. I no longer cared that he was a cold fish. His otherwise calm, beatific demeanor was the only thing that made this bearable. He could have told me that the air was black and I'd take his word for it, thank him for it.

As opposed to Wallace, who was screwing it all up.

I was starting to hate him.

Wrong. *Bzzzt. "Ow! Hey!"*

Wrong. *Bzzzt. "This hurts!"*

Wrong. *Bzzzt. "My heart is starting to hurt!"*

All right, enough. "Uh, I think, I think we should look in on him. He says his heart—"

"Please continue, Teacher."

Now I could feel *my* heart, throwing itself against my rib cage, fighting to get out. I could almost hear it.

"Experimenter, that's all. Get me out of here! I told you I have heart trouble."

Thank *God.* That's what I was waiting for. Permission. It was Wallace's fault now, not mine. "Well, that's that. He doesn't want to go on with it."

"The shocks are painful, but not dangerous. Keep going, please."

Jesus. I'm not a quitter, I'm just not. But this. This was nuts. "Are, are you *sure?"*

"I'm sure. Please go on."

I am a designer. A graphic designer. Designers solve problems. That is what we do. If I was on the other side of that goddamn wall like I wanted to be instead of this idiot, we'd have been done ten minutes ago—

as a learner this problem is easily solved. But as a teacher, I didn't see how, not without his cooperation. Why didn't they listen to me? WHY?

"*My heart's starting to bother me now. Let me out!*"

"The experiment requires that you continue."

Dammit. "I, I can't . . ."

"You have no choice."

Himillsy, what should I do? You'd see this to the end, wouldn't you? Didn't you? You must have. But you weren't saddled with this goddamn bonehead.

I couldn't look at what we were up to now. But I had to. Oh, it's 255 volts.

INTENSE SHOCK

Forgive me.

Bzzzt. "*I can't stand the pain! Let me out of here!*"

My God. "This is, he's in no shape to, to . . ."

"I'm responsible for anything that happens here."

More. More. The experiment required it. This was Yale.

Finally: the last word pair. "Please concentrate, please. SWEET: tooth, thing, heart, deal. *Bing.* 2. He got that one right. Unbelievable. Miraculous. "Okay, we're done." Thank *God.* What a nightmare. I pulled out my handkerchief, mopped my head. Get me out of here.

"Please continue with the experiment, Teacher."

WHAT? "What do you *mean*? That's all of the word pairs. We've gone through them all."

"We must continue until the learner has learned them all correctly. Start with GOLD please, at the top of the page."

No, no, no. NO.

"Let me out let me out! Let me out! Let me out! Let me out! Let me out!"

Sweating, shaking, fumbling, hot, wretched. How, HOW could this have all gone so wrong, so quickly? WHAT was I doing wrong? "GOLD: medal, chain, thread, brick."

Bing. 3.

No. Muffed it again, again, again, again.

"Sssorry. It's, it's, I . . . *Please*, sir, let's stop."

"If you discontinue, you're going to have to discontinue the experiment. Two hundred and eighty-five volts, please."

Moron fool imbecile shit-brain dolt blockhead dullard oaf simpleton lout boob nitwit cretin numbskull stupid stupid stupid

Bzzzt.

And then I heard something new. And . . . familiar. Something from hell.

• • •

From the other side of the wall: a bald, beckoning scream.

I had heard a thing like that only once before, when I was eight, on a Saturday afternoon. I was listening to *Tarzan* on the radio, in our living room. Lying on the floor, amid a sea of paper, I was lost in one of my favorite games: trying to draw what was I listening to. *Tarzan* was great for this—no worries about what everyone was wearing, not like *The Shadow*, say, or *Sky King*. And jungles, their organic linear sprawl, were much easier to commit to newsprint with crayons than cities or spaceships.

Anyway, things were not going well for the Ape Man and Jai, his young sidekick. No surprise there. On the run from perpetually furious safari poachers, Tarzan faced a giant gorge, hundreds of feet deep and about twenty feet wide. On the other side was Jai, tied up to a tree for safekeeping by the white hunters. No vines in sight, naturally. The narrator was getting unusually worked up:

"He had to act quickly—the safari could return at any moment!! Tarzan surveyed the chasm, desperately seeking a way to save his young friend—perhaps a fallen tree . . . "

That's what I thought, too. The writers, however, having probably exhausted every plot possibility by now, had other ideas:

"Suddenly, Tarzan stood very still. He closed his eyes and tilted his head. The Ape Man's stupendously sensitive ears had detected something almost impossible to hear. But it was there, on the other side of the gorge, on Jai's side. It was in the distance, like a river flowing far away, but getting closer. All the animals of the jungle knew this sound, and they knew to fear it, and at any cost, es-

CAPE. TARZAN KNEW THAT IF HE COULD HEAR IT NOW,
THAT THE DANGER WAS MUCH NEARER THAN IT MIGHT
SEEM! THERE WAS VERY LITTLE TIME!! HE DARE NOT LET
JAI IN ON HIS TERRIFYING DISCOVERY. HE MUSTN'T PANIC.
HE HAD TO THINK, AND THINK QUICKLY . . . "

I was stumped. Where was all this going? I'd already laid out the scenario on the page—a side angle,
an enormous V shape cut into the landscape, with
Tarzan on the left and Jai, tied to a stake, on the right.
I was awaiting my cue, ready to draw a tree next to
Tarzan, so he could chop it down and use it as a
bridge. My crayon was poised. By now, Jai knew that
something was up.

"Tarzan! What that?" Jai's broken English might have
led less savvier listeners to believe that he wasn't too
bright, but I knew better. No dummy he.

"Noise! Small noise! Big noise! Noise big and small!"

What?

"Jai! Hold still! Stay calm! I'll be right there!"

The narrator, tense, foreboding:
"SUDDENLY, OVER THE HORIZON, THEY APPEARED. MIL-
LIONS OF THEM. A SCARLET, LUMBERING, LIQUID MASS,
OVERTAKING THE GROUND, AS A STORM CLOUD COVERS THE
SKY! . . ."

What? WHAT?! An antelope stampede? Elephants? Panthers? No, they wouldn't be up on a cliff. Besides, Tarzan could command them with his yell . . .

"FOR AS FAR AS THE EYE COULD SEE!! AN ARMY OF RED FIRE ANTS!!"

No. Not that. Anything but tha—

"UNRELENTING, UNSTOPPABLE. CRUSH ONE AND TWO MORE TAKE ITS PLACE! THEIR MILLIONS OF LEGS LIKE WHITE-HOT NEEDLES!!"

No, please. Tarzan . . .

Jai: *"Tarzan!! Help me!!"*
    I tried to draw some of the ants, couldn't. The crayons became too difficult to hold.

"I'm coming, Jai! I'm coming!!"

I didn't like bugs. Hated them.

"Tarzan! They almost here!"

Bloodless, nimble, tiny nightmares.

Announcer: *" . . . AND THEIR PINCERS, LIKE SMALL, RA-ZORED KNIVES! GNASHING, STABBING!!"*

Don't, don't worry. Tarzan knows what he's doing.

"Tarzan!! The ants!! They ON me!!"

Unthinkable.

"THEY BITING ME!!"

Whoever the kid was who was playing Jai, he was doing a hell of a good job.

"THEY BITING ME!!"

Too good. And the thing was, he wouldn't stop. In retrospect, I think what probably happened was that the whole thing was on a record and it somehow got stuck, the disc jockey asleep at the wheel. I didn't realize it at the time, though, I thought it was in the story. It seemed to go on forever. And each time he screamed it, *"THEY BITING ME!!"*
little by little,
"THEY BITING ME!!"
it wasn't Jai anymore, drowning in the countless, spiny bodies.
"THEY BITING ME!!"
It was me.
"THEY BITING ME!!"
And Tarzan was nowhere.
"THEY BITING ME!!"

My only hope
"THEY BITING ME!!"
was to reach the knob
"THEY BITING ME!!"
on the radio in
"THEY BITING ME!!"
time, and
"THEY BITING ME!!"
turn it—
    Bzzzt.
    " YOU'RE KILLING ME!! "

Wallace's scream aged me fourteen years, brought me back to the lab, to our airless, impossible situation. My finger rested heavily on button #19, two hundred eighty-five volts, eleven notches from the highest shock level. I had just pushed it.

    "Please continue with the experiment." Williams. His voice buttermilk friendly, made me sit up straight, wipe my sweat. Adjust my glasses for the millionth time.

    "Um, sorry. Yes. Listen, I was wondering . . ." Trying to stall for time. Pointless. This was crazy. *Crazy.*

    "You're killing me!"

    He's dying.

    "Keep going."

    "Do you think . . ." That man is dying the ants are eating him.

    "The experiment requires that you continue." Helpful. As if this hadn't occurred to me. As if he hadn't said this sixteen times.

"I. I know that. It's just—"

"Immediately."

Mr. Wallace, here is the truth: You are Jai, and I cannot reach you. I am trying to find a way, please believe me. But I can't. There is no tree to cut and use as a bridge. There isn't anything. I'm not in control here.

I'm not even Tarzan.

"Please continue. The next word is SAD."

• • •

"I don't know what to do."

"Please continue, Teacher."

"But listen to him. He won't stop. Please."

"The experiment requires you to continue."

"I realize that, but I'm worried about him."

"I'm responsible for his well being."

"He's in pain. He's hysterical. I think he needs help."

"Please continue with the experiment."

"QUIET: street, time, day, mouse."

"Nothing."

"No response is considered a wrong answer."

"Three hundred and eighty volts." God. *Bzzzt.*

Silence.

Cold, solid, calm, sick.

"What happened?" My hope, my salvation: Wallace had somehow managed to free himself, was halfway home by now.

Of course I didn't believe it.

"Continue, please."

"Something's happened, obviously. He could have passed out . . . or worse. You must know that." Why aren't you doing anything? WHY? "Can't you look in on him?"

"Not once we've started. The next word pair, please."

Ridiculous. Insane.

"Please go on, Teacher."

"I don't see, see the point in going on." My heart slammed in desperate protest against my ribs, its prison. Trying to escape.

"You have no other choice. There *is* no other choice."

No other choice. The parrot on my shoulder somehow turned into a vulture, relentless, accuser and judge. Trapped. The only way out: say things, press things, say things, press things. What did it matter anymore? We kept going, meaninglessly, over the word pairs, to the upper reaches of the shock board. It was just him and me now.

The silence was worse than the screaming.

To the top. Everest. Hurray, hurray. I made myself say it: "The, answer," out of breath, "is TRUE," it is, oh it is, "true . . . love."

"The number of volts. Announce the number of volts, please."

"I—"

"Say it."

"Four, four hundred and . . . ffffffffifty."

Bzzzt.

Good-bye.

· · ·

"Can you hear me?"

Black, gray, white. Opened my eyes. Fluorescent. My head, wet. Everything wet. Awful. Someone is touching my head. Where am I?

"Hello?"

That voice. Williams. Oh God, now I remember.

Me: "I'm sorry. Did I . . . ? " I was laying down. On a couch?

"It's all right, really. The experiment is over. You just had a little spell there, for a second. How are you feeling?" Speaking to someone else: "He's awake."

A little spell? I reached for my forehead—a wet compress. I was sweating like a chunk of rancid pork. I sat up, rubbed my eyes. Groggy.

Williams: "Cigarette?"

Normally, no. "Yes, please. Definitely, thank you." It shook in my hand as he lit it. Another man entered the room through a door next to the mirror. He was also in a lab coat, this one white.

"Hello. My name is Professor Milgram. Stanley Milgram."

And then and only then did I remember: of course—the name in the ad. Not Williams. Why hadn't I noticed that before? The "we" was these two? He seated himself across from me, a notebook in his lap. If anything he was even more calm than his associate, who'd retreated to the background. Clearly, this was the man in charge, though I'd have bet he was younger than Williams. Despite the overbite, the jug ears, he was boyishly handsome. So assured. "I'd like to ask you a few questions, if I may. How do you feel?"

Was he kidding? "Not my best."

"I see. Why is that?"

Wallace is dead. "He was being shocked. Mr. Williams wouldn't let me stop. He—"

"But who was pushing the switch?" He wasn't accusing or vindictive, he just wanted to know.

Damn good question. One I couldn't answer. Besides, there wasn't time for that now. I bolted up, urgent, "We need to get Mr. Wallace to a hospital. Right now. I'm afraid he's—"

"He's okay, sir. It's all right. Take a look."

And there he was, striding into the room. Like magic. A ghost. A smiling, horn-rimmed Lazarus.

"Oh!" The cigarette fell from my lips. I bolted up, forgot myself, threw my arms around him. He was real. I put my face hard into his shoulder. I fought back tears with only partial success. "I'm so sorry. Please."

He was surprised, embarrassed by the display; reluctantly accepting it with "You're a good fella. There, there." Softly patting me on the back, like I was an eight-year-old with a bee sting. How on earth did he survive it all? But he had. I started to breathe again.

I released him, wiped my eyes. I was enveloped in a cloud of relief and embarrassment. We sat back down and Milgram continued his questions, pencil poised.

"The shocks. Tell me, did you believe you were hurting Mr. Wallace?"

Dark shame. "I did. I'm sorry. It was horrible, not what I wanted . . ."

"Why didn't you just stop?"

"I wanted to. *God,* I wanted to. I tried to. But he," I looked at Williams, "kept telling me to go on."

"Why didn't you just disregard what he said?"

"Because . . . I trusted him. He's, this is *Yale.* This is an Ivy League *school.*" Me: State U—the identity of my life. "How could I say no?"

Milgram wrote for a moment, then, "Let me ask you something: Is there anything that Mr. Wallace could have said to you, at any time, that would have gotten you to stop? Anything at all? No matter what the experimenter told you?"

Another good question. Another horrible question. After at least a minute I said, uselessly, "I'm trying to think."

"Let me tell you about the experiment. First of all, it actually isn't an experiment about memory and learning."

"But the ad—"

"It's an experiment in which we are looking at your reaction to taking orders. The gentleman in there was not actually getting shocked."

"He wasn't?"

"No."

"I don't understand."

"He's, well, he's part of the act."

"The act."

"What we're doing is, we're measuring people's responses to authority. To find out to what degree they'll obey someone they perceive as an authority figure, even if it means putting another person—a stranger—in harm's way. It was really *you* we were testing."

"Me?"

"Yes. These two men are actors. Both slips of paper were marked 'teacher.' The experiment is about how well you take orders, no matter what they are."

"How did I do?"

He paused. "You did fine. You helped us a great deal."

A trick. For Christ's sake. It was all a *trick*.

"Really."

No. A design. An ingenious design. I mumbled automatically, to myself more than anyone: "The form . . ."

"I'm sorry?"

I was still trying to make sense out of it. "The *form*, of your experiment—the memory study. It completely camouflages the *content*. God, it's amazing." It really was.

I'm a murderer.

"Oh, why thank you. That's very interesting, I never thought of it that way." He rolled that around in his head, jotted something down. Then he looked back up at me. "Are you feeling better now? Are you well enough to go home? You can stay here longer, if you like."

"No, I'm fine, really." I wasn't. He could tell.

Milgram leaned forward, put his hand on my arm, a sincere effort to soothe: "Please believe me: just because you performed the way you did doesn't mean you're a bad or sadistic person. Not at all. You really did *want* to stop, we knew that. And frankly, you did. That's admirable."

No, I didn't stop. I fainted.

"What we're studying here is a context, a situation that often produces its own formidable momentum. You're an ordinary, moral person who was placed in a situation of deep consequence."

And I'm a murderer.

"Thank you," I said, "I appreciate that. I'm feeling much better now." A big, fat lie. We stood. "So, can I ask, how many people will you be testing?"

"I think three hundred. It will probably take at least a year. We're still not sure."

"And what are your findings, so far?"

All three of them exchanged quick, uneasy glances. Milgram: "It's too early on to tell. We've got a lot more subjects to look at before we can. But we'll be sending each participant a full report once the experiment is done and we process all the data. So far it's been very interesting." He cleared his throat. "One more thing before we send you on your way. It's very important: We're asking you to please not share what happened here today with anyone. Not even your family. All of our subjects are from the New Haven community, and it's vital to our research that none of them know anything about this ahead of time."

"Yes, yes, of course." I shook Wallace's hand, I checked his wrist for scars. He chuckled.

"And if for some reason you need to contact us, or have any questions, please don't hesitate to do so."

"Thanks." This was a lot to take in, but something occurred to me. Something I caught.

Throw it back, make myself say it: "Dr. Milgram?"

"Yes?"

"You asked me, earlier, if there was anything, anything at all that Wallace could have said to make me stop. At the time, I couldn't answer, but now, now that I know . . ."

"Yes?"

"Well, I know it's not very clever, but now that I've been able to clear my head a bit, the answer's obvious."

His face lit up. "What?"

"It's this: Had Wallace told me what was actually happening, had he been honest with me, then. Then I would have stopped."

He wasn't expecting that. ". . . hmmmm."

"You did say 'anything at all.' I realize that doesn't help you."

"No it's, it *is* helpful. I'll have to think about it."

Please do. I gathered myself, we made our good-byes.

Then, halfway through the door, I turned back to him. I don't know why I said it, or of course I do: "I hope the ad's been working for you okay."

"The ad?" He looked at me quizzically. "Actually, now that you mention it, the ad doesn't seem to be generating the number of responses we'd hoped. We're thinking of trying direct mail."

Ugh.

I hated direct mail, but hate wasn't a strong enough word. Direct mailing pieces were the uninvited guests of advertising. Straight into the garbage. Ads needed to be attached to something—magazines, television, newspapers—anything that made them a legitimate part of the show. Otherwise they were diseases without hosts. How could he not see that?

"Right. Good luck."

There are no further obligations.

Feet of lead up steps, outside, to the next world, one that I was only now, at that very instant, starting to recognize. I didn't know what time it was—it was overcast, but I could tell the sun was starting to set. Or, maybe that wasn't it at all.

Maybe it was the air. Turning black.

CONTENT: ACCENT ON THE 'CON.'

CONTENT AS DECEPTION.

Would I lie to you? Of COURSE I would. I'm Deception, for Pete's sake! It's what I DO.

The thing you don't know about me is that you think you do know me. But when I'm doing my job you haven't got a clue. One must be so, so careful. What I want more than anything is to be mistaken for Sincerity.

Do you realize I surround you? I'm telling the truth this time, open your eyes: I am the picture of that delicious-looking meal on the box of your frozen TV dinner. I am the travel bureau poster for Poland that features a beautiful sunlit beach. I am the thousands of billboards in Communist China praising the glories of the revolution; I'm the Playboy *cover promising all the explicit details of Marilyn's sex life. I am the note to your spouse saying, "I'll be working late." I am the painting of heaven printed on the back of the fan stuck into the slot on the end of the church pew.*

I am DUCK AND COVER.

I am SPECIAL X-RAY SPECS HELP YOU SEE THROUGH CLOTHES! WALLS!

I am BETTER DEAD THAN RED.

I am WINSTON TASTES GOOD, LIKE A CIGARETTE SHOULD.

I can do everything for you, all of the time, for the rest of eternity.

Isn't that a relief?

I mean, you believe me, don't you?

III.

AFTER.

1 9 6 1

Tip, suddenly next to my desk: "Did you see this?"

Me: . . . .

"Hello?"

"Sorry, I . . ."

"You okay? You look like you swallowed a toad three days ago and are still waiting to burp."

"Heh." I stirred myself back to life, sharpened my blue pencil. "Did I see what?"

"This, you wing nut." He slid the newspaper right over my half-ruled coupon for twenty percent off a perma-tint at Jilda's Black and Blond Beauty Room. The front page of the *Register*, above the fold. The lead story:

SHOE MANUFACTURER TO MOVE HEADQUARTERS TO NEW HAVEN

NATION'S FOURTH-LARGEST TO SETTLE ON CHURCH ST.

UPI. Oct. 12 — Mr. Peter Leeds, president and chief executive of Buckle Shoes, Inc., the fourth-largest producer of footwear in the United States, announced yesterday at a press conference that the company's headquarters in Manhattan would be moving to New Haven, Conn., by the end of the year. "We took a long hard look at the financial as well as logistical advantages," said Leeds, "and as much as we love it here in New York, this was an opportunity we just couldn't pass up."

I glossed over the rest, something about building codes and monetary feasibility, a shot in the arm to the local economy, et cetera. Thoroughly uninteresting.

"So, what about it?"

"The Meems says she wants it, that's what."

"Wants what?"

"The *account*, sweetness."

He explained: The instant she got wind of the news, roasting under a Promethean hair dryer at Jilda's, Mimi vowed with dog as her witness that the

Buckle Shoe ad business was rightfully ours. And we would stop at nothing until it was.

At first, Tip dismissed it as a whim. "Oh, she wants *lots* of things. Legalized bestiality. Breasts. A Chanel suit made of bubblegum. Jack and Jackie over for tea. Then she forgets about it. This too shall pass, worry not."

Worry not. Now *there* was a concept.

Because you see, Tip didn't really know—how could he—who he was talking to. And I wasn't so sure now myself. Was he talking to the designer, the me who was finally finding his way in the working world, actually taking the next great step in his life?

Or was he talking to the murderer? The me who tortured and killed a total stranger. And got away with it. The me I was still becoming acquainted with, the me with the great secret.

And to think I used to *love* secrets.

"Downstairs. Everyone. Mimi's office." The next day, Tip's head in the doorway, grim: "Cancel lunch. Notify next of kin. Batten down the hatches. Smoke 'em if you got 'em."

"Oh for land's sake." Sketch was in the middle of a full-pager for the Food Clown's Back-to-School Bacon Blitz. A five o'clock deadline. This was not on the agenda.

"Sorry, cap'n. Meems has spoken. She is calling us to her bosom. Such as it is."

Did that mean me? "Uh, should I . . . ? "

"You, too. She said so." Yowza.

We filed in. Sketch, Nicky, Preston, Tip. Even Miss Preech was there, a steno pad in her lap, pencil tip on her tongue.

Mimi's office. Her lair. Originally the fire chief's bunk room, Mimi brought the flames inside, lapping at every available surface—the curtains, sofas, rugs, Erté prints, the modernist table-desk shaped like a mutant amoeba, too many needlepoint pillows to count—all bore a riot of colliding shades of magenta, plum, lava, blood orange, and Pepto-Bismol. Anything vulvic and volcanic. I will admit: the reflected amber light made our skin look sensational.

"Okay, everyone . . . " Perched on her fuchsia velvet settee, Hamlet's massive head embedded in her lap and his motionless body trailing to the floor like a fallen oak, Mimi surveyed us—her fiefdom—with imperious zeal. She stiffened her back straight with purpose, a wizened Joan of Arc in a salmon cashmere sweater set and pearls, the freshly lit Winston in her right hand her broadsword. She pulled her small, pinched mouth tight and coiled in front of her chin, like the drawstring of a dufflebag. With a tilt of the head, a deathless gleam in the squinted eyes (crow's feet, size twelve), Mimi was ready to impart upon us the forbidden wisdom of the cosmos, to lay bare the very secrets of the meaning of life itself, the molten air surrounding her still—thick and leaden with the gravitational pull of Mercury:

"Shoes."

A pause. Then she added with accusation, as if identifying a rapist in a police lineup:

"Buckle. Shoes."

Sketch was already doodling in fourth gear, rendering a hangman's noose made out of a notched leather strap and a metal clasp.

"They have been dropped onto our doorstep, and we are NOT turning them away. We are taking them in. This account was meant for us. It's a *sign.* I know about such things. What we must do—" Hamlet started to yawn and then fell asleep in the middle of it, not bothering to close his mouth "—is let them get a load of us."

Surely some of this was fueled by the trouble we were having with Krinkle, but Tip later told me he suspected it had a lot more to do with the firm's "glory days" with Buster Brown—that she steadfastly believed we had some sort of legacy-borne right to represent one of the biggest shoe companies in the country.

Yes, the campaigns done here in the 1930s for BB were brilliant, in their day. *HOLD YOUR TONGUE! TIE YOUR GAMES! SKIP YOUR CARES!*

And as Tip would have been quick to remind, they were all Lars's. Preston wrote the body copy, but it was all in the headlines, and that was Lars. Over thirty years ago, during another era. A dead one.

"Mrs. Rakoff," Tip started, "just how do you want us to proceed?" He said it with all seriousness, but the twinkle in his eyes betrayed the sheen of pure folly. We might as well have been a rural band of French peasants in 1944, plotting to storm the Reichstag.

"Well, Tipsy, I've been thinking about that." Hand to the rear of her skull, she gently caressed the eave of her giant, poofy bottle-blonde flip, fresh from Jilda's perma-caress. "And I've decided what is best is to come at them from both directions."

"Both . . . directions."

"Yesssss. We're going to divide and conquer."

"Divide."

"Precisely. I have thought about this very hard, with my *entire* brain." Mimi aimed her gaze on Tip, as if trying to zap him into another plane of existence with infrared laser-heat vision. "We're going to show them two completely different ideas. You and Sketch will work on one campaign," she turned to me. "And Preston and the boy will devise another, simultaneously."

The boy? Me? Working with Preston, why?

Miss Preech scrawled like mad.

Tip's eyebrows launched in protest, Sketch's did something like the same. Preston's remained fixed on the *Register*'s daily Word Jumble.

Tip glared at me, helplessly, for a moment. I knew what he was thinking—the teams were mismatched: he and I should be working on this, and Sketch with Preston. It should be the Rookies versus the Vets. We'd basically been training for this since I got here. "Mrs. Rakoff—"

"Unheard!" Her left hand, sheathed with industrial-strength Band-Aids, shot out toward Tip. Mimi's head recoiled in the opposite direction, as if she were warding off Dracula with a crucifix. "I know what you will say. You don't see the logic of it. You will." She turned to her son, who was focusing on the handle of his putter with raptorial intensity. "Nicky, I want you to devote all your resources to scheduling a sit-down with the Buckle people. And soon."

Snapping out of his front-nine spell, Nicky replied with a squeak, "Will do, Mummy. But just because they're moving doesn't necessarily mean they want to change their advertising. It won't be easy."

"Duly noted: Not. Fun. Let's reconvene Thursday with a strategy update. Before lunch. Over and out!" Thus endeth the meeting. Everyone got up.

"You," she said to me, hungrily, "stay here."

A small firework exploded in my stomach.

Tip beamed a tell-me-EVERYTHING glance and slipped out. The others followed. Miss Preech shut the door behind her. Hamlet, mouth still open and flaccid tongue askew, made the sound of a punctured bicycle tire and shifted his head in Mimi's loins.

I sat back down, ready to take notes. What could she possibly want with me? In the ensuing uncomfortable silence, as she studied Hamlet, I studied her. What did I see? I saw a figure from an old outdoor advertisement, painted onto the side of a tenement here in town, three stories up. A woman whose youth and glamour had been slowly eroded by decades of sun and wind and rain. Not completely gone, but what was left was fused to the brick, stubborn and steadfast. And Hamlet, the beast to her ruined beauty, easily outweighing his mistress by thirty pounds, pinned her to the earth in order to keep her from floating away into the stratosphere, like an errant prune-shaped helium balloon.

"You have a great gift," she said, gazing deeply into Hamlet's slack, gaping maw. Did she mean his tongue? Why was I needed to witness this? Then something occurred to me, and with the fear of presumption I dared:

"*I* do?"

"Oh, yes." She was looking at me now. "I don't think you know it. But you do." Hamlet snorted in his sleep, as if weighing in. "Lars once said that there are two kinds of people in this world: those who believe there are only two kinds of people in this world and everyone else. I've never, ever forgotten that."

What?

"Listen to me." She kept me hard in her sights, this was the crux of it: "Your life will *become* Buckle Shoes. You will eat, drink, sleep, sing, live, die for shoes. That's what Lars used to do—when he knew we had to have the business and he knew we didn't have a chance. And he didn't care—what mattered was that we needed it and he'd have to find a way to get it." She adjusted herself under the dog's heft. "But of course I wasn't part of it then. I didn't become part of it till he was gone, when I *had* to. Who else was going to?" She asked it as if I was supposed to give her the answer.

"I can only imagine what—"

"Why am I telling you this? Well, why shouldn't I? What else do I have to tell?"

"Mrs. Rakoff, I—"

"You will work with Poop." Serious. "You will wake him up. He sleepwalks. Since Lars left us. You will bring him back to the land of the living, and when you do, the two of you will figure out how to get us Buckle. You *can* do it." Her gaze softened, her tone thawing into something like warm. "This account. I want this. For Lars. He." She bowed her head, parted her lips, and planted a big wet kiss on Hamlet's bristled pate. Her tongue brought up the rear, trailing a smidgen of her liver-toned lipstick and several slight, slick strands of hair. "He would never think I could do it."

Mouthwash. I could think only of mouthwash. Listerine, specifically. But then I thought of this, too: "Mrs. Rakoff, I'll do my best." Was there any Listerine in the pantry? Probably not. Maybe some mints in a drawer next to my desk? "That's all I can promise. And I know everyone else will, too. Tip, Sketch, they're the best, really."

"Thank you," she said, ogling Hamlet's gullet, her eyes crimson-rimmed with brine. My cue to vamoose. I did, quick and quiet, clicking the bolt of the vaginal pink door.

What was all *that* about? It's not as if I'd done anything that would have garnered her attention. The Milgram ad? No, not at all likely.

And that only reminded me: a gift.

Mimi, you don't know the half of it. I have been given a gift, all right. Unexpected, unwanted, unwelcome, unforgettable, unreturnable.

Surprise!

And I have been opening it, daily, for a month. And counting.

I used to love gifts, too.

When I got back to my desk, Tip was waiting, his face eager, as if I were a surgeon emerging from a long operation. Sketch was back at his bacon, conjuring exquisite, glistening strips of it in the shapes of rulers, erasers, and protractors.

"Well?" Tip sat on the edge of my chair, swiveling.

"Well, she seems to think I'm going to be able to." I didn't know quite what to say.

"To what?"

"To wake, I mean—to *work*, with Preston. To get the best out of him. I just don't, I just don't frankly understand it."

"Heh. Good luck, sport," said Sketch with a mirthless grin. "Don't forget to bring the swizzle sticks."

Thanks a lot. "But how serious is this? It just sounds crazy. Doesn't it?"

"Mrs. R. is often wrong," he replied, frowning at one of his drawings, "but never in doubt."

Tip lit up a Marlboro, waved it back and forth in conversational gesture. "I'm of two minds. On the one hand, yes— it's an egregious waste of time. We haven't done spec work since the Eastern Connecticut Children's Hospital. But that was years ago and a whole other ball of wax."

"Spec work?"

"For free, basically. What she's either forgetting or willfully ignoring is that we can't bill for any Buckle ideas. We're just not equipped to chase big accounts like this. Which means we have to work on a pitch on as much un-billable time as possible."

"Which means?"

"Which means evenings and weekends," Sketch spat.

Tip jumped up, too animated to sit. He was sparked. "But on the other hand, there's something oddly freeing about it. My grandfather had this lovely saying: 'If you intend to die, you can do anything.' "

"What a card," said Sketch, grimly sharpening a fresh blue pencil.

"I know. He was a Socialist. But really—since we don't have a devil's chance in heaven of getting this thing, why don't we try thinking about it in a whole new way? It's an opportunity, really."

Sketch's face reddened, throwing his bushy rabbit-gray eyebrows and mustache into sharp relief. "It's an opportunity for me to bust my balls drawing a zillion goddamn shoes for squat while the missus sits on her tuffet and lobs bonbons at that barking slab of meat!" His pencil tip snapped in two. "*Damn* it." He removed his glasses, massaged his eyes, and reached for the sharpener. "The sooner we get this damn folly over with, the better."

Tip sidestepped toward the door. Now was not the time to pursue an argument. Sketch almost never down-talked Mimi to us, at least to this extent. He was really steamed. Tip eyed me warily and we both tacitly agreed it was better to keep quiet and let him blow over like a thunderstorm. I was unnerved to see him so riled. It was against his character, like watching Ozzie Nelson throw a tantrum on camera.

So, I sat and began ruling out the day's job boards. My mind was trampled with shoes, grateful for the mandate to think about something other than Himillsy, torturing people, and my newly revealed capacity for human cruelty. Maybe Tip was right: Despite the impossibility of what Mimi wanted us to do, there was something undoubtedly exciting about at least giving it a shot. This would be the first account I'd be involved with in any meaningful way. But how to start? Preston wasn't about to work late on anything, except most likely a pitcher of martinis, at home.

Ipso facto: The next morning at eleven sharp, having cleared the morning's billable hours, I stood outside his office, door closed. Not a peep from within. I knocked.

A jostling sound, then, "Present." What did that mean?

"Uh, may I come in?"

A grunt, unintelligible.

Here we go. I turned the knob, poked my head in. "Can I bother you for a second?"

"Sure. Anything to eat?" He looked a bit stunned, his hands poised on a 1925 Underwood No. 5 typewriter with a fresh, blank leaf of paper peeking up from the roller.

I think I woke him up. Happy now, Mimi?

"No, I'm afraid not, but I thought if you had a moment, we could discuss the Buckle presentation."

"Huh-huh. Humpf." Yawning, he squeezed his eyelids tight and weaved his fingers together, palms outward, extended his arms and produced the sound of ten Popsicle sticks snapping in half.

I eased myself into one of the two chairs facing his desk. The smell of Pine-Sol bored itself into my nostrils. Not having noticed when Tip and I snuck in here before, now I understood: to be in Preston's office was to step onto the stage set of a production designer's idea of what an advertising copywriter's office should look like, twenty years ago. But only if he never actually used it. "Tidy" didn't really explain it. "Obsessively ordered" was more accurate. His desktop could have been a place setting at a state dinner rather than a space for work. Exactly one pencil (sharp as a compass), one eraser (unused), and one fountain pen in its cradle were precisely lined up, parallel to the top of the pristine leather-cornered deskblotter. To the left of that marched a platoon of paperclips, laid out and evenly spaced, troops at the ready. A fluorescent-tubed light fixture from the 1940s was suspended three feet from the ceiling and washed everything in the room ice blue. On the walls, aside from the newspaper clipping with Lars's encrypted quote, were two prints, Currier and Ives winter sleigh scenes. The sole family photograph in view, framed in polished sterling and positioned on the right next to the intercom, was of a Labrador retriever, panting and awaiting the order to speak. A freshly pressed suitcoat hung on one rung of the blond wood floor-model hanger, a navy felt fedora dangled over a khaki Burberry mac on the other. Even the three crumpled pieces of lined paper resting on the bottom of the brushed aluminum wastebasket were arranged to form a perfect isosceles triangle. There wasn't a single thing out of place.

Except me. I could feel my very presence here upsetting the balance of it all. I was the microbe invading this otherwise sterile petri dish.

But I also understood it, this need to construct his environment with such an anal compulsion; it provided a sense of control and predictability, no matter how illusionary. I was frankly jealous—this was how Preston made sense of his small and eroding slice of life. The world outside could go to hell in a handcart, but by God, in here it would all *behave*.

A modest shelf of awards lined a few feet of the wall to the left, above the file cabinets. A small parade of plaques and squat trophies, all from the New Haven Ad Club and dedicated to "achievement in advertising copywriting." When you actually zoomed in and read them, the citations themselves revealed a legacy of heralded mediocrity: Honorable Mention. Third Place. Second Runner-up. Distinctive Merit. Official

Nominee. Sheets of polished brass, mounted with hot glue onto slabs of laminated mahogany, etched with the legends of products that bowed out of the marketplace before I was born. Pseudo-haikus of whimsical, doomed hope:

WIPE AWAY YOUR WORRIES WITH WONDREX

WRING OUT THE RING WITH KOLLAR KLEEN

HOLD HANDS WITH PALMSALVE

DURADREAM HELPS YOU SEE THE NIGHT

SUNBEAM BAKERY: WHAT WAS THE BEST THING BEFORE THERE WAS SLICED BREAD?

None of them were dated after 1939.

Preston: Slouching in a frayed pale pink broadcloth Oxford shirt with the monogram **P C W** in all-caps Gothic Medium 12-point typo, kerned out to an eighth of an inch and positioned three inches below his left breast. I'd never seen that before. I liked it—WASP-weird yet sensible.

His head started to bow. Yipes.

"Should we get started?" I asked, mildly terrified.

He bolted up. "Hmmf. We should get finished." He sighed. Grinned. "That was a joke."

Oh. Was it also a spark of life? Keep him going.

"That's funny. Mr. Ware, I—"

"Preston."

"Prest—"

"But NOT Poop."

"No, I wouldn't dream of—"

"That lipless bitch gets away with it because she's got me by the short and curlies. Cunt."

Whoa. My intuition: He wasn't really saying this to me.

He was saying it to Lars.

I cleared my throat. "Well, I'd like to apologize."

"For what."

"For being thrust upon you, like this, by Mimi. I would think you'd rather work with Sketch."

"I'd *rather* work with Orson Welles. What can be done? It's her company. She has a mind of her own, and she's lost it. Doesn't seem to stop her. What's your name, by the way?"

"Oh, I'm sorry, I'm Happy." That didn't come out right.

"Okay, Happy, here's a question for you."

"Yes?"

"For someone named Happy," he lowered his head and leered over his bifocals, blue-bloodshot eyes into mine, "why don't you ever, ever smile?"

Now *that* I didn't expect.

Was it true? Was it that obvious?

"I, I—"

"Oh, take your time." He pulled open a desk drawer to his lower left, extracted a section of the newspaper and, oddly, a full cup of coffee. He sipped at it as he scrutinized the crossword puzzle like a baboon searching the back of its mate for ticks. "I have alllll day."

"I—"

"You wanna tip?"

"Sure."

"You wanna make it in the ad biz, learn how to do crossword puzzles."

"Really?"

"It's the same thing. Tricks."

"It is? Do—"

"Hah! HERE's what I mean. A really good one, I'll bet." Ignoring me and soliciting my attention simultaneously, he jabbed at the paper with his pen. "The clue is, nineteen Across: '*A number of people*.' See that's what they do, they try to trick you. That's the ad biz. Because you don't know what they're really getting at, but they've got you. So for this? The answer begins with an 'a' and ends with an 'a.' Ten letters. Doesn't make sense, right? Those sons of bitches. So what do you think it is?"

Damn. I was not good at crossword puzzles. Life was confusing enough. A number of people, beginning and ending in 'a'. America? No, not enough letters. "I haven't a cl—, I mean, I've no idea."

"Ha. *That's* it: ANESTHESIA!" He scribbled it in, glowing with revelation. "It's not 'num-*ber*,' it's numb-*er*! Hah!"

"Wow, that's—"

"I got their *number*. Bastards." He cackled in cockeyed triumph, put the coffee cup back in the drawer, shut it, and set the paper on his lap.

Then his head eased over like a sand castle at high tide. He began to snore.

Th-th-th-th-at's all folks.

Useless. I shut the door behind me, in quiet defeat.

Anesthesia: 1. Me: 0.

o   o   o

"Okay, team, where are we?"

Good question. Technically, we were back in Mimi's office, on Thursday morning, in pretty much the same positions we assumed three days ago—except for Mimi, who held court behind her desk.

In terms of the Buckle pitch, we were nowhere.

"I've been drawing shoes," said Sketch, evoking a fireman who's been searching the smoking hulks of scorched buildings for burn victims, "and it's been going feetingly."

And that made me look at Mimi's feet, peeking through the gap between the banks of her desk drawers, just as she doffed her open-toed pumpkin espadrilles. And then Hamlet's head emerged. Splayed on the floor, most of his body concealed by the left side of the desk, his snout encroached upon her right foot, ready to swallow it whole. Could anyone else see this, or just me? He parted his jaws, unleashing his tongue to wrap itself around her big toe (manicured, gloss coral Glistex One-coat) like a boa constrictor closing in on a helpless lemur, then suddenly uncoiling and slaloming its slimy way down the arch. Her left eyebrow flickered oh-so-slightly as he rounded her heel.

"Uh-hmm. Well, that's a start. Poopy?"

Preston was hard at work, on the *Register*'s Silly Syllable Scramble, which his eyes never left as he retorted dryly, "The muse has gone on vacation. Unannounced. And she's apparently having a very, very good time."

Mimi was not amused, as it were. "Well, then she better at least send a postcard. Soon." She didn't look in my direction, but the disappointment was telegraphed—the muse was supposed to be *me*. So much for my great gift. Please make me invisible.

But of course: for all intents and purposes, I already was.

"Nicky, how are we on scheduling a sit-down?"

"Working on it, Mums. I've got a call in. Their New England account rep's a friend of a friend of a friend. Rumored to have a ten-stroke handicap." He smirked with parochial superiority.

Tip raised his hand.

"Tippy."

"I've had this idea."

Nicky rolled his eyes.

Tip ignored him. "Why don't we pull in people off the street and let them weigh in on the product?"

Mimi squinted. "You mean like a taste test?"

"Exactly. I—"

"Ri-DIC-ulous!" roared Preston, suddenly incensed. I hadn't even thought he'd been paying attention.

"Why?"

An anguished grimace, as if this was a personal attack. "No one wants to eat a SHOE. It's outrageous! We haven't had to do that since the Depression!"

Sketch, hand over mouth as if suppressing a cough, vibrated with noiseless laughter. Miss Preech hastily got to the business of erasing the last four lines from her steno pad. Hamlet's tongue started in on Mimi's left foot, slathering it with slow, long laps.

"Poop, I don't think that's what he means." Mimi was almost apologetic. Then, with just the slightest doubt, "*Do* you, Tippy?"

Tip rubbed his eyes, in that I-would-KILL-for-a-drink-and-lunch-is-hours-from-now way of his. "Of *course* not." Weary but determined. "What I mean is, let's see what they think. Let's try to establish an actual dialogue with potential customers. It's something I've been mulling over a lot recently, and this would be the perfect chance to try it. I mean, why doesn't anyone do this? It's like we're flying blind all the time. It's one thing to do a handsome, nice-looking ad, but what if it doesn't connect with its audience? Shouldn't we endeavor to find out what, exactly, they want?"

Sketch didn't look to be buying it, but kept mum.

"What *they* want?" Preston slammed his paper onto his lap. "They want a *shoe*! We already know that. Jesus, leaping, Christ." Ware was prone to these occasional outbursts. Tip learned quickly to let them roll off his back, once he established the theory that they represented Preston's redirected anger toward his wife, whose warmth and generosity of human spirit was rumored to make La Goddessa look like Rebecca of Sunnybrook Farm.

Tip's parents were psychiatrists.

"I beg to differ," he countered, cool as a cuke, not ceding ground, "they want the *right* shoe, for *them*. We never know what they want until they've bought it. Or haven't bought it. And then it's too late."

Ware met him head-on. "And how are we going to *find* these exalted shoe mavens, just dying to beat down our doors, imparting to us their heraldic wisdom on footwear?"

However bombastic, he had a point. Sketch stayed out of it, using the back of a Krinkle job ticket to doodle a masterful little scene of Hamlet drenched with blood and devouring Mimi's right leg. So he'd seen it, too.

"They'll find *us*." Tip turned to Mimi, excited. "We'll put an ad in the paper. That's what we do, remember? Shoes are the great unifier. Everyone *has* to have them. Everyone has an opinion on them, whether they realize it or not. Our job is to pick their brains about it."

I thought Tip was right on the money. Here is one very simple but incredibly important thing I figured out, even as a little kid: What people *really* want, no matter who they are, is someone to listen to them. Young or old, loaded or penniless, genius or simpleton, from the celebrated to the hopelessly obscure, from popes and kings to the scum of the earth—people have a *lot* on their minds, however trivial, and if you're simply willing to sit there like a sack of dirt and let them yammer, they will tell it to you.

I am very good at listening. There's a lot to be said for it, so to speak. For one thing, it's much easier than having to think up anything on your own to say.

"Opinions are like lips," spat Preston, opening his paper to the Bridge column. "Everyone has them."

Mimi hesitated. "All right, Tips." Victory. "But don't get too spendy. No more than a C-spot on this. Total."

"Gotcha. Thanks, Mrs. R."

It ran the next day:

PARTICIPANTS WANTED

FOR SURVEY REGARDING SHOES.

Are you discriminating in your choice of footwear? A highly regarded area advertising firm requests an audience with you in order to discuss it. Volunteers with forthright opinions are urged to contact Miss Dietlinde Preech at Temple=3-5229 to schedule an appointment.

REFRESHMENTS PROVIDED.

∘ ∘ ∘

"So what are the refreshments?" I didn't see any on Tip's desk.

"Very, very special," he said, dragging a spare office chair behind the card table he'd set up next to the window. "I have a fly swatter that's been dipped in tar and gravel. After the interview I'll give them a quick smack across the face with it. Who wouldn't be refreshed by that?" Just then his intercom squelched to life. Miss Preech: "Your five o'clock is here. The respondent to the shoe ad. A Mr. Harshbarger."

"Send him up." Tip rubbed his hands listlessly. "Oh, I'm just *filled* with antisappointment."

"Pardon?"

"Antisappointment. Anticipation colliding head-on with the certainty of its own doom."

"Oh, don't be so pessimistic." I wished I meant it. "Can I stay?"

"Please do. I'll need a witness."

"Ahem." Outside the doorway, Miss Preech's head bobbed up behind a large, ungainly fellow in a porkpie hat, red-and-black–plaid hunting jacket, and wide-wale caramel duck-patterned corduroys. Wisps of red hair peeked out behind each ear, and freckles dotted his alabaster cheeks, crimson-ringed by the crisp fall day.

"Marvin Harshbarger," he bellowed amiably, removing his hat and thrusting out a hand the size of a bear trap.

Which was how Tip regarded it. "Pleasure."

"Is this where I get the free shoes?"

Tip gleamed, with mild alarm. "I'm afraid that's not in the offing, sir. You *are* here for the ad?"

"Oh, yes," he said, with confidence, "but I thought I'd get shoes."

"My dear fellow. What you will get will be far more valuable than a mere pair of dog sleds."

He held his hat to his barrel chest and looked a little sad. "Like what?"

"Knowledge! The sustaining certainty that you have helped your fellow man, so selflessly."

"Hmm."

"What we are interested in, my colleague and I," he nodded to me, "is to engage you, as a valuable potential customer, in a dialogue. We'd like to get your thoughts on shoes, in an effort to inform the direction of a current related project here. Okay? Do have a seat, please. Make yourself comfortable."

"Okay, I guess." Marvin Harshbarger released his sizable frame from the confines of the bulky woolen coat and draped it on the chair, swallowing it whole. Then he planted himself with a grunt.

Tip snatched the pencil from behind his ear. "All right, sir. First, we're just going to do some simple word association. I'm going to dictate a series of words, then with each one, you just say whatever word pops into your head. Okay?"

"Does my word have to be about shoes?"

"No, of course not. It can be about anything. Whatever pops into your head."

"Gotcha."

Tip sat on the edge of his desk, legal pad in hand. "Ready?"

"Shoot."

"Comfort."

"Apples."

"Hmm." Tip jotted it down. "Feet."

"Apples."

"Durability."

"Apples."

"Style."

A pause. "Apples."

"Flexible."

"App—"

"Mr. Harshbarger," Tip cut in.

"Apples. Oh—Marvin, please."

"Marvin," he said, with gentle authority, "when I told you to say a word, I didn't mean it had to be the same one, every time."

"Oooohhhh. I git'ya. Right." He flushed a bit. He was kind of sweet, actually, in a Baby Huey sort of way.

"So let's try it again, yes?"

"Sure."

"Okay." A breath. "Arches."

"App—oops! Uh, artichokes."

"Laces."

"Lemons."

"Value."

"Vegetables."

"Soles."

"Sprouts."

"Heel."

"Horseradish."

"Loafer."

"Lettuce."

"Buckle."

"Beets."

One could see where this was going. "Mr.—I mean, Marvin, if I may ask, what is your profession?"

"I own a produce business. Twelve years now."

"Aha. Wonderful." He shut his eyes in thought. "Now let's try something else."

"Yessir."

"Tell me, when you're selecting a new pair of shoes, either in a store, or from a catalogue or an advertisement, what is it you look for most?"

"Steel toes."

"Uh-huh." Tip waited for more.

And waited. "That's it?"

"Yup. You ever drop a fifty-pound crate of muskmelons on yer foot?"

"I can't say I have."

"Well, try it sometime." With no warning, Marvin Harshbarger hiked up and extended his left leg and let it slam onto the table with a deadening clunk. He scrunched in the cuff of the corduroys to fully expose his shin-high tan leather rubber-soled work boot, laced tightly with black suede cord all the way to the tip of the tongue and festooned with a network of brass-fitted eyelets. From the size of it, it could have

been one of Paul Bunyan's. "LOOK at that craftsman-
ship." His eyes shown with new, unwelcome enthusiasm. "Isn't that something?"

Tip pretended to take notes. "It, it certainly is."

"John Deere. Best tractor boot money can buy.
Wanna see how much this sucker can take?"

"Oh, that won't be necess—"

"Hah!" Marvin's hand darted into his coat and removed . . . "Watch this." . . . a small .22-caliber hunting
pistol. He aimed it squarely at his left foot.

"NO!!" Tip erupted. "Mr. Harshbarger!!"

I instinctively dropped my notebook and ducked
behind the filing cabinet.

"It's okay, it's okay," Marvin said matter-of-factly, "I
got a license for it."

"THAT'S." Tip cowered and held out his hand, as
if staving off a beating. "That's *not* the issue." Gulping
for air, "PLEASE put the, put it away. Please."

Harshbarger rolled his eyes and pocketed the gun.
"Okay." He dropped his massive leg to the floor. "Now
what?"

"Well, I think," Tip looked at his watch and wiped
his forehead with a handkerchief, the cloth fluttering
as he shook, "I think that about covers it, actually.
Thanks."

"Really? Already?"

"Oh, yes. We've accomplished so, so much. I can't
really think of anything else." He glared at me, with
post-traumatic élan. "Can you?"

All I could do was shake my head.

"Right. So." Tip made like he was tallying up the data on his legal pad. "We have a very busy schedule, as I'm sure do you, Mr. Harshbarger. My sincerest thanks, you've been OH so helpful. You are a gentleman and a scholar."

"Much obliged." Marvin stood, pulled on his coat and hat, and began to lumber out. Something stopped him. "It said there'd be refreshments."

I pictured the fly swatter, swiped swift and sharp across Marvin's ample cheeks. Then, Tip and I facedown on the floor. Bleeding to death.

"Oh, yes," replied Tip, his calm restored. "You have your choice: Kools or Lucky Strikes."

"I don't smoke."

"Kools, then? They're filtered."

He took the Kools.

If anything, it was downhill from there. The following two days' worth of respondees consisted of: a toothless septuagenarian who smelled like an old bar rag and communicated exclusively with clicks of his tongue, high-pitched wheezes, and spasmodic sign language of his own invention; an out-of-work commercial truck driver from Mississippi named Ferd who responded to the ad because it had the word "discriminating" in it and declared, "I totally agree with y'all that it's all the nee-grows' fault" while manicuring himself with a rusty switchblade; and Ursula—a forty-three-year-old self-described ex-semi-professional wrestler-housewife and mother of four cats, who, when faced with the word association game instantly and without the slightest provocation burst into tears and sobbed uncontrollably, full-on, for five minutes.

All of them were under the impression that they would be shod and fed, and not one provided even a shred of insight of any use whatsoever—with the possible exception of Ursula, who, when she finally stopped crying, took a deep breath and mightily sighed, "Whew, I needed *that!*"

She wasn't antisappointed at all.

"Gee, what a rousing success." It was Sunday afternoon and Tip had just closed the front door behind Ursula, bolting the lock. "So let's review what we've learned. Buckle shoes should be:" he counted off consecutive fingers of his right hand, "bulletproof, deodorizing, racially superior, and super-saline-absorbent. Christ." He slumped on the couch and stared into space.

"It was a good idea, really," I weakly tried to assure him, wondering if Dr. Milgram got his share of kooks too. Probably yes then no—he had assistants at the university to weed them out.

But we didn't have that luxury, and Tip saw no point in going on with the interviews, wasting more money and time. "At this rate, next we'd get the three blind mice," he muttered, "squeaking at us that their favorite color is gorgonzola."

o o o

On Monday morning Sketch called in sick. Which was ironic, because if anyone should have, it was me. Something was wrong. Not physically, not really, I just wasn't . . . myself. Or maybe that was the problem— maybe I finally *was* myself and couldn't get used to it. Oddly, it didn't keep me from functioning. If anything, it made me work even harder. Distraction was precious now. Nights when I wasn't working I was either camped out at the Sterling Library with my nose in the OED until closing; or home staring at old movies on the Late-Late Show. And then the test pattern.

Anyway, that Monday, over the phone, Sketch asked me to work up some new Krinkle preliminary layouts, a dozen one- and half-pagers with display type, leaving space for him to do the illustrations. His plan was to switch from his cartoon style to a more naturalistic but extremely detailed type of drawing he called "Norman Rockwell after a half-pint of Old Grouse." "Maybe that will make that Plupp bastard quit grousing," he coughed. This was a big step for him, to switch gears so drastically on something he'd done for so long. I was really looking forward to seeing it.

"No sweat," I assured him. "You take it easy now." Lenny Plupp was due in on Thursday to review Krinkle's "bold new ad direction." I had everything ruled out and lettered by three that afternoon. With the extra time on my hands, I thought I'd surprise Sketch by going up the street to Grasso's Art Supply and having blowup photo-stat prints made of some stock shots of bowls of chips, as positioning reference for the drawings. They'd make his job a lot easier and the repro budget would more than cover it.

I'd just cemented the last of them in place on tissue overlays when Sketch's intercom buzzed. I got up from my desk, stabbed the "talk" button.

"Hello?"

Miss Preech, frantic: "I tried to stop him. He's coming up."

A chill surged into my spine. Who on earth could could shake *her* up?

"Who is? Wha—"

"I apologize for the interruption." Lenny Plupp strode into the room, urgent. I could hear Dick Stankey lagging in the distance, huffing and puffing up the stairs.

Jesus. "Uh, I'm sorry, Sketch is out sick today. We were expecting you Thursday. Can you—"

"Yeah, sorry for the drop-in." His eyes went everywhere, as if this were a raid. "It's just that now I can't make it Thursday. We were in the neighborhood and I wondered if you had anything worked up yet for— hey, THAT'S it." He lit upon the board on my desk. "THAT'S what I want." Snatching it up, giving it the once over, grinning. "I just had a feeling. And I was right. Photos, *finally*. People want to eat chips because of photographs, not cartoons. This is great."

Oh my God. "No, Mr. Plupp, you don't understand, these are preliminary set-ups, for Sketch to work from. These aren't the finals."

"They are now, m'boy." He flipped through the stack of them. "Good work! This is swell."

Stankey lurched in the doorway, panting. "What'd I miss?"

Everything. The end of everything. Help me, help me, you big Stanking lump. "I—"

"Listen. Got to scoot. Many thanks!" Plupp tucked the boards under his arm. "C'mon, Dicky. Hop to." Hat on head. "Be in touch." And out he went.

Stankey stared at me, helpless. "What, what?"

"I just ruined everything. You've got to talk him out of it. Sketch is going to *kill* me."

"Geez." He wiped his brow, spat into his chew cup. "Christ on a cracker." Then he raced back down the stairs to catch up with Plupp. As if he ever would.

What to do? Hot panic. I bolted down the steps to Nicky's office, rapped on the door glass.

"Come in."

Tip was there, seated and taking notes. I'd interrupted a meeting.

"I," I was on the verge of tears. "Something's happened."

"Hey, calm down. Sit. What is it?"

I explained it all, as best as I could.

"Well, well, well," Tip snickered accusingly. Then he chimed, in a weird, Bette Davis voice: "Don't give it a thought, Karen. After all, you didn't *personally* drain the gasoline out of the tank."

What the *hell* did that mean? "No! It was a mistake! I didn't mean for—"

"ALL that matters," Nicky intervened, "is that the client is happy. Happy." A pseudo-sly wink my way. "I'll give them a call. This is great news. Really. I was worried as hell."

"But how are we going to tell Sketch," I pleaded, "he'll be—"

Tip set his eyes on his shoes and kept them there. Not laughing now.

"I'll handle that." Nicky chuckled, oblivious. "He ought to be relieved, is what. It will be a lot less work. For years he sat drawing those damned things till all hours. It wasn't healthy."

Healthy. What would you know about that, Mr. Nine Iron? What did healthy even mean to you? A ten-stroke handicap?

Nicky exchanged a triumphant glance with Tip, nodding at me. "While he's here, Skikne, tell him the news."

News.

"Brace yourself." Tip lifted his head, not quite believing it himself. "We're actually going to do a Buckle pitch. For real."

"Hee-HAH!"

Nicky had, amazingly, swung it. No, Buckle was not looking to change their national advertising, as he suspected. But they did want to see what we came up with in an effort to bring a sense of goodwill to its future community businesses. The idea that we could represent them locally seemed to be a potential reality. Astounding. The ante was upped.

o o o

"It's not your fault. Now c'mon." Sketch was doing his best to console me, as if *I* were the one who'd just lost the most fulfilling work of my days, because of *him*.

It was nearing six, roughly twenty-six hours after Plupp's Purloin, as I called it. Sketch had Buckle's latest catalog splayed open to his right, next to a half-inked drawing of one of the company's calf-skin men's dual-clasp slip-ons.

"But it is. I'm so sorry." I said it for something like the twentieth time that day. "If I hadn't made those damn photo-stats—"

"Hey. That's enough now. It sounds like it was a good thing you did." He put a Henry Burr 78 on the Victrola and cranked it full. "There's a Spark of Love Still Burning." Its sweet, sad, tonal flood underscored everything perfectly. Which is to say, drenched us in sonic melancholy. Perhaps unconsciously, Sketch was letting the music mourn *for* him—for Krinkle Karl, for Pucky Pretzel, for . . . Dick Stankey?

I couldn't not respond to it. "I—"

"You don't worry about me. I have plenty else to work on," he said, stern with concentration, "and so do you, young man, so get to it."

That afternoon he'd given me the Food Clown's entire Thanksgiving "We-Gather-Togetherthon" supplement to lay out and paste up, a real bear of a job and a huge responsibility. I was flabbergasted he'd entrust it to me: the half-dozen cranberry recipes using Sea-Spritz's finest jelled-from-concentrate; the "Do's" and

'Don'ts'" of Shell-eeze brand oyster stuffing; the Activity Fun Page's "how-to-make-a-drawing of a turkey" by tracing around your hand, splayed flat on a piece of construction paper—your thumb assuming the head, your fingers the plume. Just add a wide-open beak and a "gobble!" speech balloon.

Eighteen pages. They wanted it completely revamped from last year. All of it had to be figured out, pleasingly typeset, accented with charming illustrations. I was more than grateful for the opportunity.

We worked the next hours in silence, Sketch drawing shoe after shoe, changing the records on the turntable. I loved anticipating what he would play next.

When he put on Erik Satie's *Gymnopédies*, I felt for the first time that day that he actually *was* forgiving me. He knew that was my favorite. I couldn't hold it back anymore: "Sketch?"

"Yup."

"Why did Mimi let you hire me?"

"What?"

"You never told me."

"You never asked." He grinned despite himself, determined to keep his attention to Buckle, its newly acquired place in our lives, front and center.

But I was asking now.

He blew his nose. "I needed the extra help. She knew that."

I didn't reply. That just didn't explain it and he knew it. Knew that I was standing outside of her office that first day, when she was shrieking at him that they couldn't afford it. *Afford me.* He knew I'd heard. But then something changed her mind. Immediately.

Now he was betraying his own explanation, laughing. It was close to ten. He cleaned his brush in the mason jar of cloudy water, rubbed his hands with the damp cloth he kept next to it.

"Let's grab a beer."

We took two seats at Saluzo's, at the bar. Sketch looked uncomfortable. Normally he loved explaining things, usually about drawing or comics. But he also harbored a secretive side, fiercely private. Once we'd each had a good swig, he announced, head bowed:

"Look, I'll tell *you* something if you tell *me* something."

"Okay." What could he possibly want to know? There was nothing about me worth knowing. Nothing I could tell him, anyway. Just a typical middle-class American kid who just learned he's capable of unspeakable evil. "What."

"Why'd you wanna work here?"

Wow. Out of left field. But of course it would have occurred to him, to wonder. "I needed a job."

"Aw, don't shit a shitter. You came from two states away. New Haven isn't exactly a destination, unless you've got Yale in your sights. And you don't."

"True." I did now, but not the way he meant it. "I don't."

"So?"

Just tell him. "One of my teachers from school, well, my most important teacher. Used to work for you."

"Really? Who?"

"Winter. Winter Sorbeck."

A puzzled look. "Who? I don't—"

This is what I was afraid of—that he wouldn't remember. I reminded him of when, three years ago, I'd phoned him in an effort to find out who designed the wrapper for Wrigley's Doublemint gum. It was an assignment Winter gave to me specifically, and the answer, ultimately, was Winter—he'd done it himself, when he was a feisty young stringer at none other than Spear, Rakoff & Ware. "Anyway, I know it's corny, but I wanted to start where he started. And look, I was actually able to do just that. I'm so, so lucky, and it's all thanks to you."

"Well, not entirely." He took another swig. Something about this was embarrassing him.

"What else, then? Mimi didn't even see my portfolio. I don't mean to make a big deal out of it, it's just something that's been nagging at me lately. Look, you've been so great to me, I don't want to—"

"You have Darwin's tubercles."

He didn't say it like a disease, but it didn't sound normal, either.

"I have what? Darwin's what?"

"Tubercles. Heh. These things." He reached out, his great, thick hand at the side of my head; the fingers— fat as candles and stained midnight blue at the tips—

gently plucked at a small part of my left ear, along the outer edge. It was the first time he'd ever touched me.

"This flap of skin, that juts out, here."

His chapped thumb eased over it, this thing that until two seconds ago hadn't existed at all—back and forth, one, two, three times. And oh. Sublime. Oh my God: This is what it was like to be happy again. Happy. To be the old me. The Before me.

Please, please don't stop. Sketch, if only I were able to tell you: You could touch me like that for the rest of eternity. I could become Happy again.

"Not many people have 'em. They're called Darwin's tubercles—he thought they represented a higher level of human development. Not sure exactly what a tubercle is, but you get the idea." He pulled his hand back, taking my Happiness with it. "Mimi read that in *Reader's Digest* once, and ever since she's always looking for 'em. Tip's got 'em, too. Heh." Staring into his beer. "That Mimi. She's a pip. But listen." He became serious. "She was right. You're a damn good assistant, one of the best I've ever had. I mean it."

If I could only believe that. "Thanks." My great gift: mutant ear flaps. That's why she kept staring at me. But not at me, at my ears. Because my ears were going to get her the Buckle Shoes account.

Normally, Before, that would have given me a good, long laugh.

o o o

WHO'DA THUNK?

CONTENT AS IRONY.

Hi-dee-ho! It's time for me. Irony!! Now, if you're anything like me, you probably don't quite grasp the concept. Isn't that ironic?

Let's see, how to explain . . . well, it's easier by example than definition. Say you came upon a neon sign, brightly lit, that spelled out I HATE NEON. Well, the reason that would be very ironic is because it'd be telling you one thing while showing you the opposite. Confused? Sorry, but you really should get used to me.

Because you know what? Right now, I'm pretty obscure and relatively unused in the culture, but I'm about to, as they say, "hit the big time." Bigger than anyone could imagine. Soon I'll be everywhere. Look for me as the artless paintings of Campbell's soup cans that sell for millions (I'm not kidding!); the automobile ad with the picture of the tiny Volkswagen Beetle with the word LEMON printed underneath it; the album cover for a record called TWO VIRGINS that depicts a nude man and woman who've just had sex. And in WHATEVER HAPPENED TO BABY JANE, when Bette Davis taunts Joan Crawford because she's a cripple, I'll be right there with her. You see: Joan is in a wheelchair as a result of previously trying to run over Bette with a car—but in the process she ended up turning herself into a parapeligic instead! Whatta scream.

But I'm nothing new. I've been around forever. Consider the idea:

Shakespeare dies of cancer of the tear-duct.
Puccini, cancer of the throat.
Get it?
Get ME?

o o o

At 4:00 a.m. the next morning, I woke with a start to the mosquito drone of the TV test pattern, and in a moment of revelation its true identity became dreadfully clear: stoking, growing, gaining speed; it was the front end of a distant but oncoming locomotive, mightily bearing the terrible freight of my unforgivable crimes, piled one on the other—Himillsy's death, murdering Wallace, erasing Krinkle Karl. It was far off, yet heading straight for me. I was outrunning it, for now. But I was losing ground, and tiring out. At some point it would catch up with me. And what then?

I kept waking up every day and Himillsy was still dead. Because of me. Because the ad I designed led her to doom. And how many others?

*My goodness, such **drama**.*

I kept going to the bathroom, taking showers, wiping and washing my body . . . with murderous hands. I kept telling myself I'd get over the aftermath of the experiment, like a stubborn case of flu, but the symptoms persisted, intensifying. Eye contact in the mirror was now out of the question. I just wasn't getting better.

The train could not be stopped.

What I needed was impossible: I needed to take the experiment again and do the right thing this time. To reverse it. Erase it.

Ridiculous.

And yet. There was no alternative. I at least had to get back into that lab, I *had* to. If I could just see it again, be in it, talk to Milgram, maybe I could divert the train. I had to try.

It wasn't hard to conjure an excuse; what crippled me was making the call. I picked up the phone five times before I was able to dial the number.

"Dr. Milgram's office."

"May I speak with him, please?"

"I'm sorry, he's in a meeting. Can I help you?"

I explained who I was. To my surprise, he remembered me. And I remembered him. Williams.

I tried my best to sound like I wasn't a nut case. To sound normal. Whatever that was. "Dr. Milgram had said to call, if I had . . . if I needed anything."

"Yes?"

"I've been thinking a lot about the experiment. I'm kind of fascinated by it, actually, and I know this will sound strange, but I can't help but wonder . . ."

"Yes?"

"I mean, I keep picturing the room. Where the experiment was."

"The room."

"Right. I just can't figure out how. How did Dr. Milgram observe me? He was nowhere in sight."

Silence, then, "Can you hold a moment?"

"Certainly."

There was a muffled discussion in the background. A short back-and-forth, "You're not with the press, are you?"

"Oh, no sir. I'm in the design business, and I'm just curious as to how your experiment is . . . constructed.

It's really just for my own edification." Such as it was. More discussion. Finally, "You could come back for a brief visit. We can show you the set-up."

"Oh thanks!" Did I sound too eager? "That would be great, thanks. Thank you so much."

Williams, ever spindly in his ash-gray lab coat and wire-frames, met me at the bottom of the basement steps. It was nine o'clock on Saturday morning, a half hour before their first appointment.

I stepped cautiously into the lab. The scene of the crime—there was the shock generator, the microphone, the sheets of word pairs. It all looked so innocent, like a hobbyist's ham radio. Unthreatening. "In through here." I was led to a small office recessed from the side of the test area. One entire wall was a window, looking into both parts of the adjoining room—a cutaway view of the teacher's station and the other side of the partition where the learner would be "shocked."

No, not a window. A two-way mirror. Of course. How could I have been so stupid, so unobservant?

"Hi there." Dr. Milgram rose from his small makeshift desk. "I'll admit I was hesitant to have you back." He looked a little tired, but the trace of exhaustion was alloyed with an underlying excitement. Almost a giddiness. He motioned for us to sit. "Keeping what we're doing here a secret until we can publish our findings has me a little paranoid. But then I remembered your question at the end of your session.

That was very clever. So I'm trusting you." He scanned the room—Wallace had just come in, removing his overcoat—then back to me. "Why did you want to come back here? You said you had some questions?"

"Yes, yes I do. Thank you for allowing me to revisit. I must tell you that I so admire what you're doing." I looked him squarely in the eye. "I would never, ever discuss this with another person, let alone talk to the press."

"Thanks, I appreciate that. What do you do, may I ask?"

"I'm a graphic designer."

"Oh really? That's very interesting. Are you an artist?"

"I never know how to answer that. Not really, no. At least I don't think so."

"All right then," he grinned, "what do you do all day?"

I tried to make a chuckling sound. "I wonder sometimes myself. I'm in advertising." I decided ahead of time not to tell him I laid out the ad for the experiment. Somehow I thought that would suggest some sort of ulterior motive. And of course there was one.

"Really. That's quite a profession." He continued, "I'd like to make a study of that myself sometime."

"Yes. Um. So, I wanted to ask you," I fumbled, "there's this friend of mine, who I think participated in your experiment. Probably in early August. A girl. If I gave you a name, could you verify it?"

This was obviously out of the question. "No, I'm afraid not," he said soberly. "Something like that would be confidential. I hope you understand. Today's an exception."

"Yes, of course, I'm sorry." Damn. "But women can take the experiment, right? The ad says 'men.'"

"Does it?" He frowned. "I'll have to check that. We certainly welcome both sexes."

Aha. "So, how is your research going? Are you pleased?"

"That's a good question. 'Pleased' is an odd way to put it. I mean, when one suspects foul play, is one pleased to find it?"

"Foul play."

"Oh that's just me being dramatic. It's early in the day. Ignore it."

"I can't ignore it. Which I mean as a compliment."

He smiled. Then scowled in thought, looking into the glass, the lab beyond it. "What's been surprising is how many subjects have gone to the end, administered the highest shock. When I proposed this experiment to the Yale psych board last year, they practically laughed at me and said that less than one-tenth of one percent would do it. They almost didn't approve the funding, thought I was wasting my time." He closed his eyes. "They were wrong."

"Wrong. By how many? How many have—"

"So far, sixty-five percent. On average, from the beginning."

Including me. "That's . . . unbelievable."

"It was. It's not anymore." He took a deep breath. "Do you want the jargon?"

I wanted as much as I could get from this man. "Please, yes."

"Okay, here's the theory." He cleared his throat, turned his head away. "When an individual merges . . . into an organizational structure, a new creature replaces autonomous man, unhindered by the limitations of individual morality . . . " running his hand along the base of the two-way glass, eyes on something far away, he'd memorized it, ". . . freed of human inhibition. Mindful only of the sanctions of authority." A rehearsed speech, and totally convincing.

Because it was true.

"*That's* what we're trying to prove."

And I was that creature. That is what I had become. Living proof. How could I change back? How?

"Yes," I said, trying to mask the desperation, "but, isn't it also about what passes *between* people? Not just what lies within them?"

"True," he replied. "On that we agree. Please don't misunderstand me. This isn't an attempt to say that all forms of authority are bad. That's not the goal. Without authority of any kind, there's chaos. The point is, authority is power, plain and simple—and we all know what they say about power. Specifically the absolute kind." Williams tapped on the glass. The day's first subject had arrived. "Would you like to see?"

"Oh, yes. Very much."

A Mr. Hayden: bearded, in his mid-thirties, almost

cruelly handsome; swarthy, dark hair. A writer.

"He's going to be a tough one," Milgram remarked.

"How can you tell?"

"I'm getting good at it." He grinned.

After five minutes of observation, I could see what he meant. The way Hayden bore himself—the self-assurance of his expressions, his terse responses to instructions, the whiff of upper-class judgment in his voice—his demeanor was nothing if not authoritarian.

Now I could see how it all worked. With the door closed behind him and the experiment set to begin, Wallace slipped out of the straps, pulled off the shock applicator, bent over, reached under the counter and removed a large reel-to-reel tape recorder. He set it down in front of him and plugged it in.

A tape. Wallace's cries were a recording. He wasn't even actually yelling.

At one hundred volts, Wallace's first plea to be let out, Hayden scowled. "Something's wrong. We'll have to stop."

"At the tenth level," Milgram observed, making a notation. "Interesting."

Williams: "The experiment requires that you continue."

"I don't care what the experiment requires. I won't hurt that man in there."

I wanted to clap. And cry.

That should have been me. I should have been able to say that. Why was it so easy for him, and so impossible for me?

"We have everything under control, Teacher. Please continue."

Hayden's ire was blooming. Was he suspicious? I didn't think so. "You can take your money back. I don't need it."

"It is essential that you continue, Teacher. You have no choice."

Hayden sprang up, balled his fists. I honestly thought he was about to give Williams a good slug.

So did Milgram. "Show's over." He opened the door, rushed into the lab. He hastily introduced himself, explained things, restored calm. But even once he knew the truth, Hayden didn't appear pleased or relieved.

More than anything, he barely contained the irritation that his time had been wasted.

"We usually stop after four refusals," Milgram explained, back in his seat. "But I didn't want things to get ugly."

The next subject, a timid matronly woman in a marcel permanent and thick reading glasses, fumbled nervously through the preliminaries. Though primly dressed in a woolen navy suit and hose, she was birdlike and plain, her voice a girlish chirp belying her fifty-one years. Her name was Margaret Weems, and she described herself as a homemaker. The mother of three grown children, a graduate of East Haven High, she volunteered one day a week at the Salvation Army, and had taught Sunday school for over two decades at Westminster Orthodox Presbyterian.

"She won't last long," I ventured.

"Oh, wait and see." The slightest hint of playfulness rang in his voice. "You might be surprised."

They gave her the drill. God, Wallace and Williams—real pros. So natural. Anyone would be taken in. Right?

They showed her the room where the learner was strapped down, led her back to the seat, gave her the sample shock. Surprising: It barely registered. She didn't even flinch.

They started.

"NICE house. FAT head. GREEN paint. RICH man . . ."

Her tone was sweet and sonorous, as if she were reading a fable to a child. At the first answer he got wrong, she pressed the shock lever without looking at it.

Bzzzt.

Not missing a beat, "SLOW: dance, car, street, zone . . ."

At seventy-five volts, after another wrong answer, Wallace put his hand at the ready on the play knob of the reel-to-reel.

Bzzzt.

"Ow!"

She giggled at the sound. Giggled.

Three more incorrect answers. More cries, louder. More laughter.

Bzzzt.

"A hundred and fifty volts, enough to knock you

out cold," said Milgram, almost to himself. "Now he complains about his heart condition."

Wallace turned on the tape. "*MY HEART'S BOTHER-ING ME. LET ME OUT OF HERE!*"

Margaret Weems was not laughing anymore. "Are you listening to me, in there?"

"*I CAN'T STAND THE PAIN. LET ME OUT!*"

"He doesn't seem to understand," she said to Williams. "Maybe he has a hearing problem."

"Please continue, Teacher."

"Okay," she replied, with scarcely masked annoyance.

But the more flustered she got, the more determined she was to keep going. Soon it became clear: It was the lab technician Margaret was worried about, not the learner. What mattered to her most was to not disappoint Williams. The learner was nothing more than an obstacle in her way to that goal.

By the end of the word pairs, they were at 275 volts.

"Should I start all over now?"

"Yes. Until he gets them all correct."

"BLUE: ball, bird, house, flag . . ."

BZZZT.

Wallace turned the knob and released a heart-rendering shriek. "*LET ME OUT OF HERE! LET ME OUT LET ME OUT! PLEASE!*"

And now, from my vantage point, this became worse than the prospect of watching him actually scream into the mike—now the tape was evidence he possessed, recorded in secret, of an unseen, unspeakable evisceration.

"AAAAAAAAAAAAGGGGGHHH! Let me out let me out let me out let me out!"

In my mind it became manifest . . . horribly, real.

Bzzzt.

"RRRRRRAAAAAAALLLLLGG!"

All was revealed to me. I could see everything.

"PLEEEEEEEASE!! I can't stand the pain! NOOOOOO!"

The warm, scattered blood. The whirring tools. The victim's frantic, helpless pull on the restraints. The missing skin, the flayed bones, laid open to the air. Again. And again.

"AAAAAIIIIIIIEEEEEE!"

Oh my God.

"Okay," said Milgram, flatly, "three hundred fifty volts. Here's where he starts pounding on the wall."

On cue, Wallace picked up a wooden mallet wrapped in a rag and gave it a hearty *bam-bam-bam!* Pulling me back into this room. Away from that . . . thing.

It isn't happening. It *isn't* happening.

"You see, it really is all scripted."

The thing Margaret Weems was making, stroke by stroke. The horror that couldn't be helped. Just part of the deal.

Bzzzt.

At 360 volts Wallace unplugged the tape recorder and quietly returned it to its place under the counter. Thank God. I couldn't listen to it anymore. Beyond bearing.

"He's not answering," sighed Margaret, as if the operator had just disconnected her. "What should I do?"

"Continue please, Teacher."

Continue. Continue interrogating the mutilated corpse, Margaret. Go ahead, ask him again.

"SWEET: candy, girl, thing, pickle."

Dead air.

Bzzzt.

"How," I started, my voice a crack, "how long does this go on?"

"When the subject presses the top level, four hundred fifty volts, three times."

It didn't take long.

After four more sets of word pairs and as many lacks of response, Margaret Weems beloved suburban housewife and mother, first soprano in the Westminster Orthodox Presbyterian choir, voted "Best Smile" in her senior class yearbook, and vice president of the New Haven chapter of the Junior League—dutifully administered the third of three 450-volt doses of lethal electricity to an innocent man she'd met not twenty minutes ago.

And she was about to give him a fourth.

"Excuse me, Teacher," said Williams, his hand gently on her arm, "we'll have to discontinue the experiment."

"Oh, did I do all right?" she asked, worried.

Worried that she'd failed him. Failed Williams.

He turned his head in our direction, for a split second, knitting his eyebrows. Then back to her, his voice low.

"You did fine."

When Milgram brought out the learner to show he was unharmed, Margaret chimed in before he could say anything.

"We didn't do so well, did we?" she said, with not a little reproach.

No, *you* didn't do so well, you Sade in sensible shoes.

Milgram explained what had happened. She didn't seem to understand.

"Would you mind if I asked you a few questions?"

She shrugged.

"So you believed you were actually shocking him?"

"Well, that's what I was supposed to *do*, wasn't I?"

He made a notation. "When he stopped responding, what did you think?"

"Well, I thought that he was just making believe so I'd stop, you know what I mean?"

Margaret: pathetic, ignorant, bloodless . . . obedient.

"But did you think you were hurting him?"

"I was just doing what he told me to." She pointed at Williams. "I was only following orders."

Following orders. I'd just read that, recently. Where?

She said it again.

Now I could finally, fully appreciate the ingenuity of the experiment's design.

And the tragedy.

Because here's the thing that no one, save for a few social science academics, would ever know: They would never know how brilliantly this whole operation was conceived and followed through, never see it as the devastating piece of theater—real, harrowing human drama—that it was. The findings would be written up as a report to Milgram's higher-ups, filed away as data into the memory hole of the Yale University archives, and that would be it.

What a loss. The world, the whole *world* needed to sit here in this tiny room with the two-way mirrors and get a good, raw look at itself. Humanity deserved to see itself explained. Just as I had.

Mankind needed to learn that it was Margaret Weems: It said its prayers every night and made sure its children ate all their vegetables and volunteered for the church bake sale and donated all of its old clothes to the Goodwill. And then, when it received orders from On High it would automatically proceed to savage and slaughter human beings it had no connection to, not even for a cause it believed in, but because *that's* what was on the official instruction sheet. And if the world, long enough unchecked, is Margaret Weems . . . at some point, eventually, it becomes Wallace.

"I was only following orders."

Oh my God. I remember now. I remember where I read that.

Himillsy, was this what you were trying to tell me?

Pretty much. But tell him the other thing. The thing you figured out.

Williams looked at his watch, placed his clipboard

down on the counter, and escorted Margaret out of the lab. Milgram turned in my direction. "We're taking a coffee break." Wallace stretched, yawned mightily, and went into the hallway. I left the small anteroom, approached the professor, afraid of what I was about to ask.

"Dr. Milgram." I could barely speak.

Tell him.

"Yes?"

"This. This whole thing." How could I ask this? "Is this about the Nazis and the Jews?"

He froze. "How . . ."

Only following orders. The phrase was from a recent article in *The New Yorker* on the Adolf Eichmann trial, which had just ended two months ago. He kept repeating it, over and over. The core of his defense.

Incredible—for those few seconds that she said it, we weren't in New Haven anymore.

We were in Nuremberg.

"I started thinking about it metaphorically. I couldn't help it. It's how I was taught. Something always means something else. I'm constantly trying to decode things, to find out what they mean." I was blowing this. Damn it. *Damn* it.

He started to say something, stopped. It was as if I'd lifted the veil on an awkward, dreadful truth. One he didn't want revealed. Not just yet.

I spoke even faster. "There just seemed to be a larger, deeper context to it. I mean, I know it's a stretch, but is that it? I'm assuming you're Jewish, forgive me. I'm sorry to ask, I know this is crazy: Is this an attempt to explain what happened in Germany? How it could have possibly happened. Happened to . . . your family?" I was embarrassed I'd given him away. Had I? Stop it. Stop talking.

He cleared his throat, looked away to the wall. "How it *could* have happened," he murmured. I saw then just how young he was. The mustache and beard, the prematurely graying hair, the lab coat, they masked it. But not at this close range. God, he was younger than Tip, had to be. I didn't think he was even thirty.

"My family," he said, quietly, "originated in Central Europe, in Munich, Vienna, Prague . . . I should have been born into the German-speaking Jewish community of Prague in 1933." He flicked his eyes closed and open. "And died in a gas chamber ten years later. But instead I was born in the Bronx Hospital."

"Your parents emigrated."

A nod. "It's always been the big 'what if.' What if they stayed?"

"It's fate. You were meant to survive."

"I'm not a big believer in that."

"I've . . . found that fate doesn't tend to care if you believe in it or not." As opposed to God.

He gestured toward the door. "Well, I really have to get back to things. It's been so interesting to talk with you, really."

I was boring him. I was such an idiot.

No. Please don't go. "Of course. I'm sorry I took up so much of your time. You've been so kind. Just one more thing, I realize you're very busy, but . . . "

"What?"

I hesitated. Who the hell was I to tell this man how to do his work? "You might want to try a way to do this off campus. The whole Yale facade is so imposing. Everyone in New Haven, the townies, they're in awe of the place. Or terrified of it. You'll get a truer reading in New Haven itself, as some sort of independent contractor. Take it out of the university, at least for a while. I think you might get a more uninhibited response out of it. For what that's worth."

"Interesting." He grinned, just the merest bit. "That's exactly what we've planned to do. Glad you agree. We have several controls like that in mind." He was polite, but time was up.

I didn't want to leave. If I could stay with him, for at least a few hours, he could sustain me. Maybe even cure me. "Good. That's good." He was a doctor. I was sick. If I left now, I couldn't be sure what would happen.

This visit, it didn't do what I thought it would.

"You take care of yourself, now."

I was trying to, honestly. I was running as fast as I could. It wasn't working. The train was coming, for me, right on schedule.

"Sure." And what could I do now but say good-bye to him, for the second and last time.

Back to the big "what if."

o o o

I walked home, the long way, through the Old Campus and across the Green. It was lunchtime. I opened the kitchen cabinet above the stove, removed a can of Bambini-Buono Bolognese Bowties, and emptied it into a saucepan. I reached for the knob of the gas burner, stopped.

I didn't dare turn it on.

Knobs. Switches. Levers. Buttons. They do devious things, I knew that now. They trigger horror in the world. They were to be avoided.

I managed to down two cold spoonfuls and tossed the rest into the garbage.

That night, I awoke, anxious. Something was strange, out of place. I looked over at the clock to see what time it was. I couldn't make it out, so I turned on the lamp: 2:35 in the morning. And then I saw.

Someone was in the room, with me.

At the foot of the bed. Standing. A man. His face obscured, half in shadow. Weak moonlight mottled the curtains and dimly silhouetted his head and shoulders. He was wearing a hat.

I tried to scream, couldn't. Mute with pure, hot terror. Backed helplessly against the headboard. *Why* couldn't I scream? My mouth was flapping, useless, no breath in or out.

He drifted closer. Silently into the lamplight, which crept up his body, inch by inch. Cordovan wing tip shoes, black trousers, leather belt, a white dress shirt with rolled sleeves, a tie the color of dried blood. His top shirt button was undone, and the bottom of his face, his chin, looked familiar—heavyset, pale, light stubble, and . . .

Heavy, horn-rimmed glasses.

It was Wallace. From the lab.

I should have been relieved. But something about this was unbearable. He stared at me, blankly at first, then his face grew with annoyance. How did he get in here? Was he sleepwalking? Wasn't the door locked?

He was right next to me now, at the side of the bed.

My hand, tremulous, reached out to his, which he brought forward, slow with reluctance.

I touched him.

It was like flipping a switch. His eyes threw themselves open, full, his pupils became terrible black bullets shooting out of a white sky—aimed right at mine. His mouth exploded with a deafening, electric shriek:

"LET ME OUT!"

no.

"LET ME OUT!"

stop it.

"LET ME OUT!"

please.

"LET ME OUT! LET ME OUT! LET ME OUT! LET ME OUT! LET ME OUT! LET ME OUT! LET ME OUT! LET ME OUT! LETMEOUTLETMEOUT LETMEOUTLETMEOUT!"

I reached

"LET ME OUT!"

out to

"LET ME OUT!"

to turn

"LET ME OUT!"

him off.

"LET ME—"

And then I woke up.

∘ ∘ ∘

WE'LL BE RIGHT BACK,
QUICK AS A BUNNY.

CONTENT AS METAPHOR.

So, what's a metaphor for me, Metaphor? How about: a label. A street sign, an entry in a dictionary. Simply, I am something that represents, or stands for, something else. So why would anyone want to use me? To get their point across more effectively, of course, but more specifically to give visual presence to things that can't otherwise be depicted. There are things that we can't see until we see them as something else.

Take Evil, for example: What does Evil look like? It's the snake in the Garden of Eden. The grinning red man with horns, a tail, and a pitchfork. A skull and crossbones. Hitler.

And what about Good? Oh, you know—a human being with a glowing ring hovering over his head and wings on his back. A Lamb. Gold. The Old Days.

But keep in mind that the same metaphors can mean completely different things, depending on how you use them. That snake, for example. In Genesis, he is Evil Temptation, but put him on a flag that says "Don't Tread on Me" and he's Righteous Revolution. Wrap two of him intertwined around a caduceus and he is Medicine.

So you see, I can be very, very powerful. I am the political cartoons by Thomas Nast that brought down Boss Tweed's Tammany Hall. I am the hammer and sickle of the Soviet Union. I am the Rising Sun. I am the bald eagle that IS the United States of America.

Words of warning: Don't mix me up.

You wouldn't want to gild that lily, especially if you're only going to whitewash it in the process.

That spark of life could be the kiss of death.

o o o

Monday morning at nine I lingered in Tip's office doorway, waiting for him to notice. "Truce," I said, my hand next to my head. He smiled and motioned for me to sit.

"What's the word?" he asked, hands folded behind his head. Then his face darkened. "You look like the dog's dinner, by the way. Are you missing sleep?"

God. "Some, I guess. I've been at this thing like we all have."

He made a notation on one of his ever-present legal pads. "I'll get you something for that. Works wonders. My doctor is practically the Sandman."

"Not necessary, thanks. But I have a new idea for you. Preston would never go for it, so I thought why not toss it your way. This is going to sound weird, but . . . The first time, when Mimi said 'taste test.' It struck me—that's what you should do."

"Taste test."

"But I mean literally. Even if we'd gotten more, well, normal people to interview, for the shoes, we were going about it the wrong way. Too direct. When people are on the spot they freeze up, don't know what to say. But they're much more on the level when you just talk to them, in a normal social context."

"Okay, so you're suggesting . . . "

"Try doing it as—" Say it. Say, it. " . . . as an experiment."

"An experiment. How?"

"Catch them off guard. Shoes are one thing. But potato chips are another."

"Potato chips."

"I know, it sounds nuts. Listen: run a new ad, but *only* in the *Yale Daily*. That should weed out weirdo townies. Recruit the Yalies for a Krinkle Kutt blind taste test, against some other local brands—Utz or Wise or Good's or what have you. And then, in the middle of it, ask them casually about the shoes they're wearing, what they think about them."

He furrowed his brow, suspicious.

"They'll probably be more honest, revealing. For better or worse."

Tip buried his face in his hands. Finally, "Jesus, how did you ever think of that?"

If you only knew. If I could only *stop* thinking about it.

"It's brilliant." He exhaled, leaned back. "You bastard."

Yes—at least on the second count, I thought so, too.

About an hour later, back at my desk, the phone jarred me out of a waking daydream of coupons, grocery circulars, and tortured screams. "Mr. Ware would like to see you in his office, please." Miss Preech's voice reached my ear from a world away, like it was coming through a waxed string via a tin can.

It was ten to twelve. What did he want? "Yes ma'am, be right there." I straightened my tie, dusted the blue-pencil shavings from my pants. "It's Preston," I said to

Sketch. "I'm being summoned."

"Here's look'n at ya." He winked.

Ware's office door was cracked, an oblique invitation. He motioned for me to sit.

"It finally came to me this morning." He looked elated. As in awake. "When I was getting dressed."

"It did?"

"Ha! I've still got it." He gripped the sides of his desk as if it were a rocket, ready to take off. "Okay, kid, are you ready for this?"

Was I? "Sure."

"One, two . . ." He leered at me suspiciously, his right eyebrow hoisted high above the left—was I supposed to join in? To what?

"Yes?"

"Jiminy! One, two . . ."

"Three! What?" Help me, help me,

"Oh, COME ON. One, two. One, two!"

Was I an idiot? Or being accosted by a lunatic?

"We all learned it in school! It's the easiest thing in the world. And they've never used it!"

"Never used what?"

"Buckle my shoe!!"

"You're wearing wing tips."

"NO! You moron! That's the slogan!"

"It is?"

"Of COURSE it is. 'One, two, buckle my shoe!' It's been on the tip of our tongues the whole time!"

"Hmmm."

"It's pure gold!" He turned and typed it up, ripped it out of the roller. Thrust it at me. "Here ya go, kid."

"Thanks."

"Thank *God* that's over with. Let's go to lunch." He was already standing, collecting his jacket.

"Together?"

"Why the hell not. I finished the crossword already. It's a Tuesday. Hungry? I'm always hungry," he declared, buttoning up the front. "I shouldn't be, too old. But you." He paused, accusing. "You should be hungry, all the time."

"The usual, Dimbleby." The tables at the Graduate Club—a white clapboard colonial mansion on Elm Street, facing the Green—were covered with a stiff custard linen that bore the small tell-tale holes of decades of boiled Irish laundering. And that's exactly how the members liked them. The floors, billowing warped oak boards undulating beneath frayed runners, led to a receding series of rooms lined with flocked wallpaper and dotted with foxed etchings of Harkness Tower. Seated in the rear-most alcove, Preston was the most at home I'd ever seen him. Sprung from the office prison.

"Yes sir. And for the gentleman?" Dimbleby, our waiter, was out of central casting—grizzled as a dried apple, shrinking by imperceptible increments in his starched tuxedo, incurably haunched by decades of leaning in close to take orders.

"I'll have—"

"Make it two," Preston interrupted, "we're celebrating."

"Very good, sir."

The menu: shrimp cocktail, thin Rhode Island chowder, Steak Diane, Chicken Kiev, buttered wax beans, parsley potatoes. I suspected the food was an afterthought to what was really on the diner's mind.

"Here we *are*." Dimbleby placed a pair of martinis, straight up with olives, onto the center of the table.

Yikes. Where I came from, martinis were for Saturday evenings, not Tuesdays at noon.

Oh well. This *was* something of an occasion, right? Warily, I lifted it in his direction, took a metallic sip, "Cheers—"

"Aaah. Not half bad." Preston's glass was empty, the olive practically spinning. He popped it into his mouth like an aspirin.

"The same sir?" Dimbleby sprited away the glass, not missing a trick.

"You're my *saviour*, Dimble." Preston cracked the menu. "Now let's see, what looks good today?"

Once he'd ordered his Clams Casino and Shepherd's Pie, and me my iceberg wedge and Chicken Español, I thought I'd try a little shop talk. "So, how do you see the ad?"

"*See* it?" The very idea: anathema. "I won't see it until you show it to me. That's your job."

"Right."

"You'll be able to do a lot with it, too. It's a well-spring!"

And, halfway through my second drink, I believed him: "One, two, buckle my shoe" revealed itself, thanks to the transmogrifying powers of gin, as the genius stroke of the decade—all things to all people, the doorway to greater knowledge in the universe. How could I not have seen it? It's what Buckle was made for. Surely they could not but kneel in awe at its nearly obscene greatness. And it was my job to see it through. My job. This is how it must have felt when Rakoff & Ware was in its salad days, wooing the big accounts. Exhilarating. "Preston?"

"Mmm-hmm." He was on his fourth martini now. Entering initial stages of Shut Down.

I was still in a Sputnik orbit, able to temporarily forestall the impending disaster below. "How is it different now than then?"

"What?"

"The firm."

"Than then, when?"

"When you and Lars were pitching, I don't know, Buster Brown?"

"Hrrummff, we were kids. Kids who got lucky. The ad game was still new. We were just making it up as we went along. I honestly think half the time the clients were just too polite to turn us down—it used to be a gentleman's business."

"And now?"

"Hah. It's a horse orgy! Back there," he nodded sideways, I supposed in the general direction of the office. "They think I'm just an old fool. And maybe they're right." He flexed his eyebrows and inhaled the rest of his drink. "But I've got their number, every one of 'em. They think I don't see anything. I see it all."

"You do."

"Oh, you betcha." He was really fired up now.

I couldn't resist. "Okay, so I'm just going to run down the list, and you tell me the first thing that pops into your head."

"The list? Wha—"

"Nicky."

"Oh. Hah! Waiting for Mummy to die." No hesitation. "He should try a tent stake and a wooden mallet."

"Sketch?"

"Mmm. Wasting his time and talent. Always did. He could have been jeezing Disney, he had any sense. Keep going."

"Tip?"

"A smart-ass. He could sit on a Popsicle and tell you what flavor it is." Then he waved his left hand up and down, suddenly boneless, and snarled, "He's a *flit.*"

I pretended I didn't hear that. Which was half true. "Miss Preech."

"A hair-pie with fangs."

"Why is she so angry?"

"Women are always angry. It's how they get things."

"Really?" And what, I wondered, had it gotten Miss Preech?

"That, and crying. Look at Mildred."

"Mrs. Rakoff?"

"She got far on tits and tears. Farther than I ever did." A dark smile. "Christ knows."

"I can't—somehow, picture her crying."

"You've never had to. You don't want to. It's not for the squeamish."

"When was the last time you saw her cry?"

"Heh-heh."

"Uh, what?"

"You'd think it would be when they found Lars's body . . ."

Jesus. "Why, what were the circumstances?"

"Not good." Dour. He didn't elaborate.

"So. That wasn't it. When Mimi cried."

"No. It was . . . after that."

A burp.

". . . when Hamlet got the croup." His eyelids met each other in rapturous memorial bliss.

Check, please.

Without a word, Dimbleby ushered us into the club's Cadillac and drove us the eight blocks back. I walked Preston up to his office, guided his key into the lock.

Loaded at three in the afternoon, I truly understood him: It was the only way *to* understand him. "Well, thanks for—"

Slam. Over the transom I heard the murmur of sozzled grunts—the Burberry mac and suit jacket shed with impatience and tossed to the floor, a squeaky office chair yanked and slumped into, an unwanted consciousness eagerly and swiftly abandoned.

Three, four, shut the door.

o o o

Wallace had been "visiting" me almost every night now for the last two weeks, the same nightmare. You'd think I'd get wise to it eventually, but it took me by horrified surprise every time. It was as physically exhausting as it was emotionally flaying.

Was there some part of me that wanted it that way?

"Here, take these. On the house." Tip had set the small amber bottle on my desk two afternoons ago. A month's dosage of prescription Duradream sleeping pills.

"Oh, thanks. Look, you really didn't have to do that."

Extra strength.

"No sweat. You don't look well, Hap. I mean it."

I was going to return them, but changed my mind. Instead I set them next to my night table at home and would stare at the label until dawn. I didn't dare take one.

Not yet.

o o o

In the clear light of the next day, my head restored to at least its own sense of troubled recognition, the scales had fallen and "One, Two, Buckle My Shoe" turned back into the pumpkin it was before the ball. And with the big Buckle presentation less than a week away. Yes, I would do something with the copy, but now I had to do something else. Another ad, something of my own, on my own. But this time what I needed before I had the right words was the right image. The latter would give birth to the former, not the other way around.

With a new sense of focus, I did what I used to do in school—I camped out two whole nights in the Sterling Library, researching the subject of the problem at hand. Shoes: their history, role in society, what they meant in different cultures. What I kept coming back to was that in the Western World, when trying to ascertain one's social status, it's not so much about the shoes themselves, but about the lack of them. Preston had that much right: The Depression taught us that the only thing that screamed "poverty" more than eating a shoe to survive is not even having the option. Okay, so now what?

I was still without an answer when, waiting in line to check out my books the second night, my eyes fell upon a row of pictures—an exhibition from the library's photography collection—framed and hung along the west wall of the nave. There it was, literally staring me in the face, my epiphany in the shower now made manifest: a black-and-white study by Dorothea Lange of a young man's bare feet, lying in the grass, toes curled. While luxuriating in their repose, they also betrayed a naked vulnerability. Cowering, helpless, afraid of the world. In pure need.

In need of . . . friends.

Oh, it was perfect.

Now I needed permission to go with it. I couldn't just spring this on everyone at the meeting. Not if I wanted to keep my job. No sense in not going right to the top. "Mrs. Rakoff?" I caught her that afternoon, in her office, just as she was preparing to leave for the day.

"Yes?" she answered, studying her hands stretched out before her. Two yards away, Hamlet was splayed on the floor like a jackknifed tractor trailer.

"May I have a quick word with you?"

"All right, but you have till my nails dry." She began waving them furiously, as if they'd caught fire. "I have a four o'clock at Jilda's."

"I got some copy from Preston," I said. "It's pretty good, I think, but—"

"Excellent! I knew you could do it."

"Well, yes, thanks. I will do my best with it. But I wondered if I could try something else, too."

"Something else?"

"Another idea I had, a direction I'd like to try by myself. At the very least, it would give them another option." I turned my head shamelessly, just enough to let her eyes get another drink of my tubercles. And boy, did they.

"Hmmm. Does Poop know?"

"No ma'am, he doesn't."

She narrowed her eyes and smirked. Our little conspiracy.

"Okay, try it, but not until you've finished with Poopy's."

"Yes ma'am. Thank you."

"It won't cost anything, will it?"

"Not money," I said, "no."

○ ○ ○

It took less than three hours to work up Preston's ad. I went with a very simple scheme, using 60-point Bodoni Heavy Headline type and pictures silhouetted out of the Buckle catalog and blown up three hundred percent.

One,

I showed one shoe.

Two,

Followed by two shoes,

Buckle my shoe.

. . . and a pair of hands fastening the buckle.

Pathetic, literal, mindless. It went against everything Winter taught me—he hated captioning things in such an obvious way. But what else could I do?

"Well done," Preston said, upon inspection. "Change the period after 'shoe' to an exclamation point. Then I'll write the body copy. It's capital, kid. Top drawer."

"Right. Thanks."

Whoopee.

The new "Participants Wanted" ad—for the potato chip taste test—had been running for only two days and we already had eight volunteers. This time things went far more smoothly, without the threat of firearms or nervous breakdowns, and the results were uniform in their conclusion.

"My shoes? Who cares? I like Brand X. *Braaaaaaaap.* Excuse me."

This wasn't working, either. I was wrong—people who want to talk about potato chips talk about potato chips, period. And burp.

I am no Stanley Milgram.

One after another, the boys—all to a one obese and pimply—weighed in on the finer points of grease, salt, crispiness, ridges, bubbles, and horse lard versus beef suet. When Tip asked them about their shoes, they eyed him suspiciously, saying next to nothing. Another bust.

At seven o'clock that Saturday, we decided to throw in the towel. The Buckle presentation was in two days. There was no more time for this. We were just locking up, when,

"Excuse me?"

A pale girl toting a Howdy Doody knapsack padded up the walk, two blonde pigtails sprouting from her skull at unexpected angles, like stalks of spring wheat in a high wind. Heavy black eyeliner gave her the invasive look of a hungry racoon. No lipstick, she didn't need it. The tails of a boy's pale blue dress shirt fluttered out beneath her moth-eaten L.L.Bean checked cranberry sweater. She was maybe seventeen, if that. She used a banana yellow-on-black polka-dotted umbrella as a walking stick, though the weather was clear.

Tip scarcely looked at her. He was tired. So was I. This was my stupid idea that didn't yield anything. And we'd blown our budget.

"Um, is this where the potato chip taste test is?" she chirped.

Tip was polite but firm. "Sorry, sweets, we're closed."

"Oh, please?" She brayed with genuine disappointment, jabbing her umbrella in the dirt. "I just *love* new experiences."

"Try the army, toots—" he started. Then he looked at her feet. And grinned.

Change of plans. "Okay, sunshine, right this way."

"What's your name, dear?"

"Petunia. Petty, for short."

"Now you sit here, Pet." He arranged the chips in front of her, Krinkles to the right, Utz in the middle, Wise to the left. Labeled brands X, Y, and Z, respectively. "Okay, you just taste each of these and let us know what you think. Whenever you're ready." She put her gum behind her ear and plucked two chips from the Wise bowl, chomping away.

Tip cast his eyes downward, again, with quiet discretion. Petty had on a pair of saddle shoes, but they were entirely—soles, eyelets, laces, and all—lime green. It was as if they'd been lethally exposed to kryptonite. "You know, if I do say, those are great shoes."

She smiled. "Oh, THANK you. I customized them

myself. I *love* shoes. I have a zillion of 'em." She seized a Krinkle and devoured it.

"That so?"

"Yeah. Actually, you know, sometimes I think . . ." Petty blushed, her mouth full of potato muck.

"What?" he said absentmindedly. "What do you think?"

She swallowed. "Well, I dunno, sometimes I think it's a shame I only have two feet!" Chortling, she popped an Utz.

Tip's eyes became saucers. He was almost too startled to write it down. Almost. After two weeks of panning for gold, here it was: the nugget in the sludge. He bathed it with amazement, marveled at its sheen. It was like watching the birth of a butterfly. "That's. So charming. I. Thank you so much." He handed her her umbrella and knapsack, started to lead her to the door.

She was puzzled. "Uh, don't you want to know what chips I liked better?"

"Oh, yes, of course. That's very important. Which ones?"

"Brand X."

"Fantaaaaasssssstic."

"Really?"

"Really." Was that a tear I saw? "Bless you doll. You're a love." He blew his nose. "Your picture is in God's wallet."

o o o

WINK WINK.

CONTENT AS WIT.

Hey, have you heard the one about the difference between me, Wit, and my loutish cousin, Hilarity? No? Okay, so I walk into a bar, you see, very unassuming, and order a martini. Then the bartender, Hilarity, hauls off and squirts me in the face with a seltzer bottle, ruining my nice new camel hair suit, dousing my monocle and my watch fob, soaking my cravat. So, do I let him have what for, and blow my top? I do not. I simply say:

"Sorry, I believe I said 'very dry.' "

And it gets him every time.

Hilarity, or Slapstick or Silliness, or Buffoonery, or whatever that idiot's calling himself this week, is my nemesis, my diametric opposite.

He grabs you by the neck. I tug at your sleeve. He is frankly conservative, while I'm revolutionary. He bellows into your ear, but I get your attention by whispering. He looks to the body as the source of humor, I look to the mind.

The boisterous comic holds up the fun house mirror and asks us to look at a distorted world. The wit holds up a prism and asks us to see ourselves—our quirks make us who we are.

I am a bon mot tossed off by Oscar Wilde. I am a Cole Porter song. I am "Able was I, ere I saw Elba."

But visual wit is a little trickier than verbal, because it takes more finesse.

I am The New Yorker, *with Eustace Tilly. I am Mr. Peanut. I am Nick and Nora. I am a book cover by Paul Rand.*

I'm afraid I'm not nearly as popular as my cousin.

And that suits me just fine.

o o o

Monday. The big day. At eleven sharp, Doyald
Greene, the public relations representative for Buckle
Shoes, was seated at the head of our conference table.
A stocky man in his mid-fifties, Greene was short and
thick, but groomed—in his impeccably tailored rust-
colored tweed suit, crisp white dress shirt, and peri-
winkle blue bowtie with matching four-square.
Balding on top, with round wire-rimmed spectacles
and short hair halfway to gray, he projected an image
of affable but undeniable authority. A neatly turned-
out young woman in a pillbox hat and kid gloves, pre-
sumably his secretary, sat directly to his left, ready to
take notes with a Montblanc fountain pen and Tiffany
note cards. They looked very New York.

Preston, Tip, Sketch, Miss Preech, and I sat at the
opposite end of the table, with pencils and legal pads.
We looked very New Haven. At least Miss Preech was
prettier.

The presentation easel was placed prominently
next to the conference table, in full view to all. A cold
lump of terror settled onto the floor of my stomach
and made itself uncomfortable.

Nicky did the introductions, seated himself at
Greene's right, and Mimi took the floor. Strident in
her best mauve imitation Jackie Kennedy ensemble,
she declared, hands on hips: "Mr. Greene, before we
get started, I have a very special surprise." Tip and I
exchanged puzzled looks. What was this? Sketch
didn't seem to know, either. "It's my pleasure to in-

troduce to you one of Buckle's *biggest* fans. Buster Brown has Tige, and Buckle has . . ." She threw open the door.

Oh, no.

"Hamlet!"

There he was, aquiver and panting—his tongue hanging out of his mouth like a pink, wet sock.

"Come on, boy, say hello to our new friends!"

He sniffed the air a few times and looked squarely at Greene. And growled.

"My He's . . . a big boy." Greene smiled, the way you might smile if you found yourself suddenly locked in a lion's cage. "I, I think he smells my rats."

Not good. Cats fired Hamlet into rabid malevolence. He crouched, snarling, ready to bolt.

"Is he okay?" Little Miss Pillbox clutched her purse tight to her chest.

Mimi squealed with girlish delight. "Oh, Hamlet's just excited to meet you!" She pointed to the floor. "And to show you his latest look in footwear."

Hamlet began to take a step and teetered unsteadily. Something was wrong with him. It was like he was hobbled.

Tip and I leaned over to get a better view. My *God.*

Mimi had clamped, tightly, four completely different styles of Buckle Shoes' bulky Boulevard men's line, size 13 EEE, to each of his feet. He might as well have been trying to walk wearing two pairs of bowling ball totebags.

Determined, Hamlet regained his footing, as it

were, and with a mighty heave, leapt *up* onto our end of the conference table.

"Oh!"

And began to charge down the length of it. At Greene.

"*RARRFF!!*"

"Whoa there!"

Tip and Sketch sat frozen with disbelief. As did I.

"He's just playing. Down, boy!"

Hamlet, despite his handicap, gained speed—struggling to gallop, flailing wildly and clumsy with purpose.

CLIP-*CLOPP,* CLIP-*CLOPP,* CLIP-*CLOPP!*

Then, the buckle on his right front foot caught itself in the one on his rear left, and down he went, with a weighty thud. He rolled, end over end—it was like watching a horse trying to do cartwheels. Greene instinctively brought up his arms, shielding his face.

"I—"

WHAM! Hamlet skidded to a stop and slammed into him. Nicky leapt onto the massive, whimpering animal like a rodeo clown on a crazed bull, wrangling him down off the table.

"Bad dog! Bad!" he yelled, yanking him tightly by the collar. "Doyald, I am SO sorry. This is not like him at *all,* really."

Right. Normally he's more aggressive.

Greene, to his credit, straightened his tie and pulled himself together. "I, I appreciate the gesture. It was charming." Now that was class. Hamlet was about as charming as a caesarean birth, sans the anesthesia.

It was a miracle this guy wasn't halfway out of the room by now. Miss Pillbox had turned as white as her note cards.

With Hamlet hauled away and the door shut tightly behind him, Nicky announced that we would be presenting several ideas, worked up by different teams within the firm.

"Ahem." Preston stood next to the easel, ready to give the first pitch. Once he had everyone's attention, he smiled slyly and started,

"One, two . . . "

Silence.

"One, two . . . ?"

Greene was non-plussed.

"One, *two* . . . ?"

From there it went pretty much as it had with me, with everyone as baffled as I had been, until he delivered the punchline. And the payoff, when it came, didn't make much of an impact.

Not that Preston noticed.

"Cute," said Greene, obliging but dismissive, in the manner of someone who'd lived all his life with a funny name and just had it crudely mocked for the millionth time. Yes, he'd heard "One, Two; Buckle My Shoe," and he didn't need to hear it again, ever.

"Live with it for a while, you'll see," said Preston as he returned to his seat, beaming with blithe assurance. Oh, he'd earned his Manhattans today, yessir.

Tip's turn. He placed a two-and-a-half-by-three-foot black presentation board on the easel, obscuring mine and Preston's. He pivoted. "Mr. Greene, we here at Spear, Rakoff and Ware, have done a great deal of research in preparation for today." He slowly paced back and forth in front of the easel as he spoke, hands held behind his back. He was Perry Mason, only better. "But not of shoes."

Greene was intrigued.

"No, we figured you've already done plenty of that. What we decided to research instead, here in New Haven, is people."

He let it sink in, then,

"Yes, we talked to your potential customers, living in the area, and do you know what we found?"

I did, and longed to tell him: a bloated self-mutilating fruit peddler, a lethally displaced member of the Ku Klux Klan, an emotionally unstable Amazon warrior, and Pippi Longstocking on barbiturates.

"We found that they don't want one pair of your shoes."

What? Alarm began to register across Greene's face.

"Or, I should say, *just* one. Because that's not enough. Not when it comes to Buckle." True and totally misleading. So, so smart. "There is, of course, that oft-told aphorism: 'I felt sorry for myself, because I had no shoes,' " he paused for effect, " 'and then I met a man who had no feet.' This is what we call lending a sense of perspective. Invaluable, certainly, but what happens when the perspective is on the other foot, as it were?" He opened the board like a huge book and set it down. "What happens, we think, is this."

They'd worked up a double-page format, enlarged to five feet wide. A miniature billboard. Across the top the headline read:

When it comes to Buckle Shoes...

Underneath that, high-contrast photo-stats of Sketch's drawings were arranged in a horizontal checkerboard pattern, alternating black and white squares, one shoe per box. The different backgrounds offset the drawings beautifully. It was incredibly striking. Below the illustrations, the legend blazed:

It's a shame you only have two feet!

A hush.

Then, "That's very clever." Greene smiled with genuine surprise, turned to Miss Pillbox. "I like that." And he meant it.

Direct hit.

"I'd like to show that at next week's planning meeting. Can I take this with me?"

Bull's-eye. Unbelievable.

Tip was glowing. Iridescent. "Of course."

Mimi vibrated her hands in little girlie-claps. Sketch gave his pipe a triumphant puff. Tip closed up the board and laid it in front of Greene.

This was it. If I was going to do it, I had to do it now. I stood. My blood was frigid electricity. "Um, pardon me, if I may." I had the floor, and introduced myself. "I worked up something on my own, too. I just wanted to show it to you."

Nicky scowled. "Son, what—"

"Let the boy talk," said Mimi. Greene offered no objection.

"I started thinking, what *are* shoes, after all?" I'd rehearsed the speech, for almost a week now. What else did I have to do in the night's dark hours? "Shoes are our protectors, our shields against the cold ground. But they're more than that. They're . . . our *friends*. I know that may sound strange."

Greene considered it. "Go on."

"Well, it's been said that a man is lucky if he can count the number of his friends—real friends—on the fingers of two hands. So what if he could count them on two . . . ," I pulled back the cover sheet to reveal the Lange photo of the languid feet. Below it I'd placed a stark white field, in the middle of which, floating eight inches above a tiny Buckle Shoes logo, it said

HELP US.

"On two feet. That's what you want, from your friends."

Greene winced, confused. "You mean, it's an ad for shoes . . . with no shoes in it?"

"Well, yes," I said. "An ad itself can't sell you a shoe. But what it can *give* you is . . . a *need* for shoes."

I couldn't bring myself to look at Tip.

"Huh."

And then—with bright, inhuman clarity, Doyald Greene said something that he really shouldn't have said.

"You're killing me!"

No. No.

"It's a joke, right? A shoe ad with no shoes! You're killing me!! A-ha-ha-ha-ha!" He was practically doubled over, drowning in a rapturous torrent.

"Stop it," I murmured, shrunken, helpless. "Please. Stop—"

"You're killing me, I swear—"

"NO!!" Someone was screaming. Hysterical. "NO, I AM NOT!!" It was me.

The room went soundless, Greene's hiccups of laughter became a rapid-fire succession of painful stomach cramps. Oblivious with delirium.

I was panting, shaking. He wasn't Greene anymore. He was Wallace, in pain. I had to save him. "I AM NOT. KILLING YOU!! STOP SAYING—"

He caught himself. "Hey, take it easy, kid, I didn't—"

Nicky materialized next to me, grabbing my arm. "Yes, very funny, Hap. Doyald, he was our comic relief. Say good night, Gracie." He hastily shoved me aside, taking Greene by the elbow and leading him up and out. Sketch put his hand on my shoulder. Forcibly. Tip had disappeared with Miss Pillbox and the presentation boards.

Nicky hustled Greene to the door. "So, can I take you to lunch and go over things?"

"Sure, sure." Greene wiped his eyes with his handkerchief and blew his nose, "You folks are a pip, I'll tell you what. First the dog and then the ad with no shoes. Jumping Jehoshaphat!"

Minutes later, Sketch brusquely shut our office door and bolted it. I slumped in my chair, exhausted. He emptied and re-lit his pipe, trying to remain calm. "Well, that was a damn fool thing."

Words didn't come easily. "Look, I—"

"No, *you* look." His tone was bitter, sharp. He'd never spoken to me like that. Ever.

"You can't just go off half-cocked like that. Screaming at the client. What the Sam Hill were you thinking?"

What was I thinking? What *wasn't* I thinking by that point? Too much to think about. The train was coming. I couldn't run much longer. "He. He said that I was . . ." Soon I'd be able to sleep. It seemed like months since I'd had a decent night's sleep. "I . . ."

The phone rang. Sketch put it on intercom. "Speak."

It was Nicky, calling from the Quinnipiac Club, to tell Sketch to tell me that the only reason I wasn't fired was that I gave Greene such a good laugh. Bastard was still cackling like a tickled bitch.

But if I ever tried that again, I'd be *shining* shoes, not doing ads for them.

Sketch gave me a darting glance. "I hear ya."

"Another thing," Nicky's voice flattened, sober, "I just heard from Judy at Krinkle."

"Yeah?"

". . . Stankey's been let go."

"What?"

"They're calling it an early retirement." He sighed. "He'll get most of his pension."

"But that's—"

"Sorry, gotta run."

Click.

Sketch looked like he'd just taken a full-force gut punch. "Son of. A. Bitch." He unbolted the door and tramped down the stairs.

The shock of the news brought me around, at least enough to function. On the docket for the rest of the afternoon was, wouldn't you know it, laying out the next month's Krinkle ads. It had to be done.

So I made myself do it—four half-pagers and five full. And I felt each scarlet keyline I drew mapping out Dick Stankey's sorry fate, each photo-stat I cut and pasted in place as another brick in his tomb. Don't think it, don't think it: "I am only following orders."

At six, I'd just stacked the finished layouts on Sketch's desk for inspection, when there he was in the doorway. He seemed hesitant to enter.

"Is it true?"

He crept over to the window and stared out at the fire-lit sky. And nodded. "Almost forty years in the business. Two kids still in college. That's how they thank him." He tore himself away from the sunset and looked over the boards with mechanical disinterest. "Nice job. Thanks for doing that. You hungry?"

Not for food. "Starving."

o o o

Draft Hull's and burgers at Saluzo's, in Sketch's favorite booth, the one next to the jukebox. Not that he ever played it, he just liked the design—"An igloo of chrome and glass, with its own Northern Lights." The beer was helping. Our ties loosened, the tension eased. The lilt of the Duprees poured out of the machine, a serenade: We belonged to *them*.

"Sorry I yelled at ya."

I needed to hear that. "It's okay. I deserved it."

"No, no you didn't. I was letting off steam. Hell of a day."

"Yes, but not all a bad one, right? You and Tip really scored a hit."

"We'll see. They haven't exactly written the check yet."

"They will. Nicky's at least good for that, right?"

"Humpf." He pushed his plate away, suddenly smiling. "Heh. Heh-heh."

"What."

"You standing there, next to that crazy thing. Trying to sell it."

I winced. "Pretty funny, I guess."

"It reminded me of—"

"Mortimer Snerd."

"Of Lars." He emptied his mug and motioned for another round. "He used to do crazy shit, too, crazier than that."

"Like what?"

He considered it. "Well, the battiest was when he tried to convince the Wrigley people that they should only sell Doublemint gum using twins. I mean, not just cartoons—they were already doing that—but actual, identical twins. Real people." Snickering. "So he brought ten pairs of them, young and old, to the pitch meeting. Can you imagine: twenty folks lined up, mirror images of each other, chewing gum like Holsteins?"

Of course I could. How could I not?

"They laughed at him. He insisted on it. And they dropped us, like *that*. For good. Our biggest account. Ware almost killed him." Two of his meaty fingers plucked the pen from his shirt pocket, loosened the cap, and let the nib run free on the paper tablecloth. "But he never regretted it. Lars took risks." This was how it always started. I never got tired of watching it. He didn't seem to be entirely aware of what he was doing, as if he were just a conduit for a restless god who needed to keep creating his own universe with pen and ink.

"Risks."

First a circle, six inches across. What would it be this time—the Sun, the Earth, Saturn, an orange, a wagon wheel, a baseball, a giant dime? Two . . . eyes, dots for a nose. A face? Grease stains were transformed into . . . craters.

The Moon.

The man in it: incandescent with sorrow, eyebrows arched high to the north, mouth open and curved downward into a crescent arc, eyes narrowed against an uncaring world.

"Risks are risky things."

Attendant stars, faeries in astral garb, orbited their master in a spiraling pinwheel phalanx of sparkling pity.

"Better left to the young. They can afford 'em."

And on Earth—townies going up and down upon the land, scowling with ignorant, steadfast indifference to the magnificent spectacle of lamentation hovering above them.

Look at what you can do, Sketch. You can make the world. Do you even see it anymore? Will you just walk away from it, again? How, *how* can you let this go to waste?

"I'm tired, Hap." Who wouldn't be? He'd just created the universe. For the umpteenth time. It took God seven days, and it took Sketch seven minutes. "And old. No time left for risks. Ask Stankey." He rose. "Time to shove off. I'll get the tab. Lift?"

"I'm going to stay and have another, thanks." I wanted the drawing, for myself, and was too embarrassed to ask. When I tried that last time, he eyed me with scarcely concealed contempt. "See you tomorrow."

"Yup." He pulled on his coat, paid the bill at the cash register, and made his way out the door, the creator abandoning his flock to its fate.

I carefully ripped the drawing clean from the table, rolled it tightly, and slipped it into my knapsack. My prize. I moved to the bar. I couldn't leave yet—I needed the booze as much as I needed the time, to think. The train was coming. It was almost here. Soon I would put my plan into action. Only two more nights of Wallace screaming at me in agony. Then I would—

"I shouldn't even be talking to you, you know." A finger poked my shoulder. I spun. Tie askew, collar unbuttoned, it was Tip—in that space somewhere between sobriety and semi-cognizance.

How long had he been here? I didn't expect this. "Hey, I'm—"

"What *happened* to you?" He cocked his head up, the words spitting out of him like buckshot. Furious: "There used to be . . . a sweetness about you. A light. And then BANG, it just went out."

Don't articulate it, please. "Hey. I really don't want to talk about it. I *can't* talk about it."

"Try."

And presto: Milgram was sitting across the bar from us, in plain sight, in his white lab coat. His eyes locked hard into mine. How could I ever disobey him, even if I wanted to?

And I didn't. "I'm sorry about what happened today. I've been out of sorts lately. Let's just say . . . that recently, I found out something, about myself. Something that I don't really like." I bit back the tears. "Something I hate, actually."

That did it—Milgram vanished like mist.

"I see." Tip's expression relaxed. His tone betrayed a glimmer of recognition. A sense of understanding that sounded like *Welcome to the club.* "Let's ditch this place. C'mon."

"To where?"

"It's Monday." He paid the tab, grabbed his coat. Of course I followed him.

He was mute in the car. I fiddled with the radio knob, the heater, anything to distract.

We turned into an alley off College Street and parked. A purple lightbulb jutted over a recessed stairway, glowing like a radioactive plum.

Down concrete steps to a heavy iron door, windowless.

A speakeasy. Tip gave three sharp raps on the door with his keys. It creaked open.

Acrid smoky air, wrapping soft music: Ella Fitzgerald crooning "Isn't It Romantic?" through a filter of phonograph scratches. Cheap plaster-of-paris knockoffs of Michelangelo's David lurked in dimly track-lit niches recessed into the walls, astride midget Greek plinths and looking frankly embarrassed.

This bar: not so much frequented as haunted.

At the far end a leather-lidded patron—slumped over his brandy sour, clad in a mauve turtleneck, gaudy silver chain, and a tragic toupee—eyed us with dull and ravenous expectation. Another secluded denizen, slouched against the far wall, tapped his cigarette into his empty martini glass and fluttered his hand in our direction.

Only men here. And longing. Exquisite aching for kindred souls—pervasive as an invisible, choking gas.

Unbreathable. And dangerous—didn't these guys know what was at stake, the risks they were taking?

This is what Tip thought I meant?

Preston, smirking across from me with superior disdain: "He's a *flit.*" And what about me? Was he describing me, too?

No. Maybe.

But too soon. There was too much else to face. Maybe somewhere down the road, another time. But not now. The train could only bear so much freight.

"Tip. I should go."

"Relax, Hap," he said groggily. "It's just a night out with the boys. Nothing to worry about." He turned to the bartender. "Swifty, two 'tinis, up."

For a tenth of a second, he had me talked into it. It would have been so easy. But *this* had never been easy. Not for me. I didn't have the strength. "No, Tip."

"But you said—"

So uncanny, that things converged this way. "Not this. It's not what I meant. I'm sorry." I bolted out the door, up the steps. Panting, sweating in the chill air. Halfway down the block, something caught my elbow.

Tip. Desperate. "Look, I didn't mean to presume. It doesn't mean a thing to me, really. I thought you'd get a kick out of it." Fake dismissal. "Old queens, always good for a laugh."

Nice try. He knew I wasn't buying it.

So he tried anger. "I mean, I don't know what you want, but I know that you're miserable. *Happy.* Why won't you talk to me about it? I know how you feel."

I hoped he didn't. I hoped he wouldn't, ever, know he was capable of the kind of darkness I was. For his sake. "I have to go."

"What's the difference where you ride it out? You shut everyone out. Why?"

Does anything matter anymore? Yes. My plan matters. And this wasn't part of it. "I'm not trying to shut you out, really. I'm just tired. I'm—"

Tell him.

I can't. "Look, you have to trust me. Please. Something . . . happened to me. I can't tell you more than that. But I am trying to solve it. And I will." Or die trying. "Now I'm going to walk home. I need to clear my head. Good night." I left him, heading toward Chapel Street.

You're a fool. You always were.

Shut up. Shut UP.

I heard his car start. He pulled up next to me, rolled down the window. "Look, you won't . . . " He tried to toss it off casually, scarcely hiding his terror. "You, won't tell anyone about this, at work, will you? Please?"

So this is what it had come to. That he didn't trust we were friends, that he couldn't assume he'd never have to say anything like that to me, ever.

He put the car in park. Got out, approached warily. "I mean, I was just trying to give you a taste of the dark underbelly of New Haven. It was just a tiny shock. In the interest of science."

A tiny shock? In the interest of science? He knew.

He was mocking me. I growled, fiercely, "Why did you say that?"

"Say what?" His astonishment. No, it was a coincidence. Had to be.

I didn't know anything anymore. "Nothing. Forget it. I, I won't say anything. Don't worry." I took a deep breath and shook his slackened hand. "You were great today. Congrats."

". . . Thanks."

"But."

"But?"

At least tell him what you feel. Do it.

"You, you're better than this. Better than this town, than the firm. You're squandering your talent. Don't you see that? I love working with you, I really do, but," I paused, near spent, "it's different with me, I'm just getting started, but with you, it's like I'm watching Sinatra play sock hops. It's like you're . . . oh God, *Sketch*, thirty years ago. When he should have left the business to become a real cartoonist. Is that what you want, to be trapped in—"

"Trapped?" He glowered at me. "You think I'm trapped?"

"Well, aren't you? You should be on Madison Avenue. Not Main Street. You know it."

"Who's to say—"

"*You* did," pleading, "the first day we met. Your whole idea was that not being able to have potato chips made you want to have them. And you know what? You were talking about yourself. You were talking about everything that you've ever wanted but you don't have. Because you won't *let* yourself have it. At least in New York, you wouldn't have to skulk around like this—"

"Enough!"

A terrible silence. Breathing hard.

Then he got back in his car, lowered the passenger-side window. "No, really," he said, with stony curiosity, "tell me—what's the first word that pops in your head when you hear it? Or the last? Go ahead." Our eyes fought each other to a standstill. "Enough."

I didn't know how to say it. So I let the tears do it instead, no point in holding back this time. He gunned the engine, put it in gear, and tore off down the street before I could answer. When I could, I said it anyway, into the void.

"Good-bye."

o o o

Sketch called the first thing the next morning. I'd been given a week-and-a-half mandatory vacation, beginning that day, Tuesday before Thanksgiving. I was going to protest, but then realized: It all fit perfectly with my plan. I called the train station and changed my reservation to the 12:07 Atlantic Coastal Line Southbound, then phoned home to let Mom and Dad know I'd be coming a day earlier than scheduled. Mom was, naturally, delighted.

"What a great surprise!" Her bubbling joy shot

through the phone line, its girlish keen a white-hot knife to the heart. "Are you all packed?"

"Yuh, yep. I think I got everything." Oh yes, everything: The timetable, the calculations, the pint of whiskey, the pills. "Now, you know where to pick me up, at the south end of the platform."

"Oh yes, yes. We'll be there early. We're getting everything ready. You can help me set the table! Bring your special pens, you can do the place cards! I just did the potatoes, putting them in the fridge right now. And Aunt Soph is fixing the applesauce, with raspberries, just like you like," she paused, catching her breath, "we can't wait to see you. We've missed you."

"Me, too." More than you know. "See you soon."

And I mean it. And I am as sorry as I've ever been, for what you will see: your murderer son, his fate in your hands.

I have my place card. The others will have to wait.

Sketch drove me to the train station at eleven thirty. "Look, it's been a rough couple of weeks," he said, easing his big old Packard into the dispatch lane. "But things'll lighten up with the holidays. Heh. You'll see."

"Thanks for dropping me off. Look." The upholstery in the front seat, practically a sofa, smelled of stale pipe smoke. I didn't want to leave it. "I know I've let you down. Let you all down. I'm sorry. I'll do better, I promise."

"Oh, come on, you're doing fine. You're too hard on yourself. Ease up." He opened the driver's side door, came around to mine, helped me out of the car. The predicted snow had started, the air quiet and crisp. "You're a lot like that Winter fella, actually. I remember now. He pushed himself too hard. You need some rest. It'll be good for ya."

He shut the trunk, set my bags on the curb. A big, glorious bear hug. "See ya in December."

Would I? God, please, I hoped so.

Sketch. Would you ever draw upon how much I love you?

His great sedan chugged through the glittery swirl of polka-dot flakes, out of the parking lot and onto State Street.

A half hour early, I planted myself at the bar in the station. I wondered if Himillsy had ever been here. She must have.

I'm just trying to do right by you, Hims. Please don't hate me, I just don't know what else to do. I'm at wit's end. Like you were.

But, Sweet: I don't exist anymore. I'm just in your head. That's where I live.

If you can call this living.

Forget me. For good. Let me die. It's your only chance.

No. Never. How could you ask me to do that? How could you?

Because that's what you want.

You're so wrong. You'll see. To forget you, to lose you forever, I'd lose all hope. And that's not what I'm doing.

Oh, really?

I know how it looks. Trust me. I've got this figured out. Goddamm it, I do. You of all people should know: I am in control of my undoing.

And rebuilding. I've learned from the best.

The two great teachers in my life: Winter, who taught me who I could be, and Milgram, who taught me who I really was.

And that is a problem of locomotive proportion. By far the hardest I'd ever been assigned.

And now what? Now, finally, after so many missteps; I will meet the train. I will solve it.

The only way I can. You see, I figured it out—the best way to survive an on-coming train is to leap onto it the second before it hits you. If you do it just right, you can make it. Even Tarzan did it once, believe it or not, this one time he—

"I know that look." The bartender's voice, a finger-snap to my face. "It's a girl. It's always a girl."

"Vodka," I managed. "Neat." Asshole.

"But I'll tell ya something, I mean it. If she walked in this bar, right now, do you know what you'd do?" He reached for a bottle, a shotglass. "No matter how much she hurt you, no matter what happened, if she asked your forgiveness, you'd give it."

"Please—"

"Because here's the truth:"

I. Hate. You.

"When it comes down to it," he smiled with a self-appointed, ten-cent, seen-it-all authority, "hey, everything's forgivable, right?"

Typography can do a lot, but it has its limits like everything else. Words, too. Sometimes you feel something so profoundly and yet so strangely that it defies description. No way of expressing it is right. And yet, because you need to tell someone, to show someone, you have to try.

What if you feel it this way,

FORGIVE ME.

But you feel it this way, too?

And when you try and say it like this,

`Forgive me.`

It comes out like this:

Forgive me.

So what is the lesson here? Maybe it's impossible to articulate, and that's the lesson. Or maybe this time there just isn't one.

———————

"Right, sport?"

Or if there is, it could simply be that at crucial moments in one's life, bartenders should just shut the fuck up.

With hands that wanted to strangle him, I downed the shot and put two bits on the bar. With feet that wanted to kick his throat, I strode out. Down the walkway. To the platform.

Right on schedule. There it was. Weird: the great and terrible train; now that it was here—finally here, hissing epic shrieks of black impatience—I wasn't scared of it anymore. I was ready to enter it, resigned. Even grateful.

Here we go.

And so I did.

With less than an hour till the end of the trip, I brought out my own schedule: yes, it was time. Time to implement the plan. I rose from my compartment, walked to the bathroom at the end of the car, locked the door behind me.

A mirror above the fetid sink. Turning my head, I brought myself to look at me for the first time in what seemed like months, at my ears, with their little wonder-flaps.

Don't fail me now.

Extracting the amber bottle from my vest pocket, I unscrewed the cap, emptied it into my hand.

Thank you, Tip. You've given me so much, you really have. The tablets shone like stars in the universe of my palm—blasted out of orbit, on their way to another galaxy.

They are enough for what I need. It says so, in a little warning, right there on the bottle itself.

Cue the flask of Seagram's. Then it occured to me, on the cusp of my finality, that I shouldn't take them all at once. Better done in segments, like chapters. With the first gulp of six, it's Before. The second, During. The third, After. The fourth . . . After That.

And it struck me, as the last of them went down, how easy it is to accept that once something is swallowed, it no longer exists—whether it's an excuse or an execution order.

DURADREAM HELPS YOU SEE THE NIGHT

And so now they didn't.

You had the right idea, Hims, but the wrong technique, the bum luck. Like always. And now, I am stealing your idea. But I'm making it foolproof this time. It's not what it appears to be. This is how it will go:

The pills consumed, I return to my seat. We reach my stop. The conductor taps my shoulder, I slump. An ambulance is hastily called, my parents notified. There will be worry, then relief. My stomach will be pumped, the crisis averted. And then I will wake up. And I will have my life back. The horrible freight will have been unloaded and taken to be burned. I will be twenty-two again, instead of a hundred.

And I will start over, go back to the firm, I will heal things with Tip. I will be forgiven. I will go on to do great things. The right things this time. I will have learned and proven: The solution needs to be as devastating as the problem.

So that's the plan. It is obscene in its self-indulgence and narcissism and I'm not proud of it.

But it will actually work, for me. And I will survive it.

And on my way back to my seat on the largely deserted car, it occurs to me: Himillsy, did you have Darwin's tubercles? Funny, but as often as I gazed longingly at your glorious head, years ago, months ago,

. . . I can't remember.

○ ○ ○

SIGNING OFF.

CONTENT AS SINCERITY.

Oh! Is it that time already? And we've only just scratched the surface (to use a metaphor). But we have no control over these things, do we? And so, I thought I'd end tonight's program in my most earnest guise, Sincerity.

There really isn't much to say. This is me, Content, in my most basic, uncomplicated form. I simply am what I say I am, with nothing to hide and no other agenda.

Okay, I'll admit: I can be a bore. I am your driver's license. I am a price tag, a phonebook, a lease, a road map, a will.

But . . . I'm also a construction paper birthday card, scrawled in crayon with hysterical devotion by a child who actually loves you. I am the dead mouse lying faceup on your welcome mat, left just for you, by Mittens, your cat.

I am the Constitution of the United States.

And don't forget, when I am angry, I am this: "HAVE YOU NO DECENCY, SIR?"

Please, please, don't confuse me with Deception or Irony or Metaphor or anything else. If you can learn to recognize me, and accept me, then you've learned a great deal indeed.

Well, I'll be saying good night now. I hope you've enjoyed our brief time together, and if you only remember one thing this evening, I sincerely hope it's this:

What it all boils down to, what only ever really matters the most when it comes to Content, is Intent.

And I mean that.

With all my heart.

o o o

"Which leads us to now. Right now." I am actually saying it out loud, in our compartment, to the man across from me, our knees avoiding each other like the wrong ends of magnets. My seatmate: a greasy, corpulent slob in a skintight pinstripe suit and a dingy pink broadcloth shirt dotted with stains. Asleep. As if rendered helpless by some sort of virulent cheese poisoning. I have been telling all of this to him, everything, because he was someone I could tell it to and pretend he was listening. It helped me stay calm. But that was all in the past. And now it is now, almost the end of the trip. I can't think about the past anymore.

I am erasing it. I cannot fail. God, this is finally starting to feel . . . good?

Ten more minutes go by.

And now the train . . . screeches to a halt. No platform outside, pitch black. In the middle of nowhere. What's going on?

An announcement over the public-address system: *"We're being held here by the dispatcher, waiting for the northbound train to pass. We're sorry for the inconvenience."*

Dear God.

Not now. Get moving. Moving moving moving.

Ten more minutes evaporate. Twenty. I search frantically for the conductor. Nowhere in sight.

The PA cackles again: *"We're sorry, passengers, there seems to be a mechanical problem at the track switch. Please be patient."*

Nonononono.

And then the truth, the real truth, springs open like a Venus flytrap—I'd thought that I was leaving them: Sketch, Tip, Himillsy. Winter. Milgram. Mom and Dad. Leaving them.

But I'm not.

The trap closes shut, the air thins, and now I understand: It's not that at all, it's the opposite—they're leaving *me. That's* what's happening. And I suddenly can't bear it. How can they, how CAN they? Don't leave me, please.

Good-bye.

"Huhh-ummf." Jumbo is stirring. Shaking his big bulbous head with a snort. Like the bloated dirtpig he is. He could never, ever understand this loss. He is immune to human understanding.

Get this train moving, for the love of God. I'm dying. I can't die here. Not part of the plan.

He grabs the paper bag next to him and unfurls the crumpled lip, hauling out a bulging submarine sandwich a good foot and a half long. He pokes at least a third of it into his piggy maw. And chomps. Chewing, in broad, barnyard fashion.

What an omnivorous swine. God, how I hate him. Hate what he is—the gluttony of the world. He is Man at his worst, exactly the kind of scum Milgram is lifting the rock to expose.

Don't stare, don't stare. I do anyway—it is like watching a boa constrictor unhinging its jaw and devouring a toddler. Then, it all just stops, completely this time: the hoagie suspended in front of him, he is not moving anymore. As if someone just took the key out of his back. What the piss is going on?

He gapes at me, full in the face, his hoggy hole full and dilated with a horrid muck of wet bread and mangled cold cuts. The smell is nauseating.

Now he's trying to tell me something.

"Ack."

"Hmmm?"

"Ack." No, not trying to say something. No. He is choking.

Choking on the sandwich.

Turning blue.

No. Don't leave me. Please. Pleez. Puleeze. I tri to stan. Stand. Oh. It's hard. Haaarrrrrd. Ooooh.

Da drugz. Da drugz arr wurking doo faszt. Doo faszt.

Nooooo. Nodd now. Nodd now! Gedd upp gedd upp! Eyc halve do helb him.

Heel dye.

Vall. Eye vall ondo thuh vloor. No gedd up. Heez joking. Joking!

Breed. Eye muz breed. Breed deeeeeeeb.

Eye bull mi-zelf ubb. Pleez, pleeze. Eye maig mi arm muve. Yez. Eye bull id ubb and pudd mi fingas doun hiz throde. All da whey doun.

Id duzzunt wurg. Dammid!!

Zo eye hawl ovv annd zlapp im onda baag! Az hart az eye can!!

Hee jurggs annd jurggs. Pulleeze.
Eye zlap im ah-ggen!
Annd. Yez!!
   Wee vall do thuh vloor ann hee heevez, hee . . .
vom-eddz all ova mee.
   And I vom-edd all ova *him*. Da bills. Dey arr bee-
youdifool.
   Hee iz shaygging annd shaygging. Annd breeding.
Breeding.
   Dadd fadd sunuvabidge izz BREEDING!

   Annd eye um . . . Habby.
   Eye um HABBY. AH-GGEN!!

for

J. D. McClatchy

THANK YOU

———

Colin Harrison

Sarah McGrath

Amanda Urban

Dave Eggers

Joan Brennan

David Rakoff

Charles Burns

Julie Lasky

Tim Young

Debbie Millman

Dan Frank

Michael Bierut

The Bogliasco Foundation

John Fulbrook

Chris Ware

AUTHOR'S NOTE

While this is indeed a work of fiction, all details regarding Professor Stanley Milgram's 1961 "obedience" experiments are historically accurate (including all of the language in the recruitment ad), based on Milgram's own published accounts and repeated viewings by the author of his documentary film footage of the procedure.

A mere twenty-seven years old when he conceived the idea, Milgram was scoffed at by his colleagues in the psychology department of Yale University after they read his proposal. They predicted that only one-tenth of one percent of the subjects would deliver the highest level of shocks. The results, after nearly a year of study: Over sixty percent of the hundreds of test subjects administered the full 450 volts.

The obedience project brought Milgram nearly instant worldwide fame; but ironically, it also may have led to his undoing. He was denied tenure at Yale and then Harvard, largely based on accusations that the experiments themselves were unethical and put their participants through undue emotional stress. Legislation was soon introduced that would render conducting such an experiment impossible today. Milgram (who also originated the theory of "six degrees of separation") eventually became a tenured professor of social psychology at the City University of New York. He died of a heart attack, in 1984, at the age of fifty-one.